TARGET: INVULNERABILITY

Light could come through the Shield, *but no weapon known to man could penetrate it.* . . .

Koskinen had developed the Shield in collaboration with the Martians. From the moment of his return to earth he was in danger. . . .

Soon the whole civilized world was searching for this one man—a man armed with the greatest potential military weapon mankind had ever seen. . . .

POUL ANDERSON

SHIELD

BERKLEY BOOKS, NEW YORK

A short version of this novel appeared
serially in *Fantastic Stories of Imagination,*
June–July, 1962. Copyright © 1962,
by Ziff-Davis Publishing Company

SHIELD

A Berkley Book / published by arrangement with
the author

PRINTING HISTORY
Berkley Medallion edition / October 1974
Berkley edition / April 1982

To MARV and JEAN LARSON
hoping someday we'll be
neighbors again.

1

FOR a moment, as he looked across megalopolis, something like terror caught him. *What do I do now?*

Reddened by haze, the sun was dropping behind a Center, which bulked black against a sky where aircraft moved like glittering midges. The whole horizon was full of such unitized sub-cities and company towers. But closer at hand Koskinen saw how the skyline was an illusion. The great buildings stood well apart, separated by a huddle of warehouses, factories, low-class tenements. Tubeways knit them together, curves which soared and gleamed in the last sunshine; but underneath lay a prosaic web of streets, belts and monorails. In the early darkness below the walls, lights had already switched on, twinkling from ground-level windows, outdoor lamps, cars and trains. The silence in this room, a hundred stories up, made the spectacle unreal, a glimpse from a foreign planet.

Abruptly Koskinen turned the viewall off. The

scene in it reverted to a random flow of pastel colors. He didn't play the records which a list offered him, not even the Hawaiian surf or the Parisian cabaret which had fascinated him this morning. *Keep your shadow shows*, he thought. *I want something I can touch and taste and smell.*

Like what?

There were the hotel's own facilities, garden, swimming pools, gym, theater, bars, restaurants, almost anything he chose to buy or hire. He could afford first class, with five years' back pay in his kick. Then there was the supertown itself. Or he could catch a stratoship to a more western city, transfer to a local flyer, rent a flitter at the edge of a national park, and sleep this night beside a forest lake. Or——

What? he asked himself. *I can pay for whatever I like, except friends. And already—good Lord, I've been on my own less than twenty-four hours!—already I know how lonely it is to pay for everything.*

He reached toward the phone. "Call me up," Dave Abrams had said. "Centralia Condominium on Long Island. Here's the phone number. Our place always has room for one more, and Manhattan's only a few minutes away, a good spot for a pub crawl. At least, it was five years ago. And I'm sure I can still guarantee my mother's cheese blintzes."

Koskinen let his hand fall. Not yet. Abrams's family would want time and privacy, to get to know their son. Half a decade must have changed him. The government representative who met the crew at Goddard Field had remarked how quiet

2

they were, as if the quietness of Mars had entered them. Also, Koskinen realized wryly, pride held him back. He wasn't going to holler, "Hey, please coddle me, I haven't got any playmates"—not after his boasts about all the things he was going to do back on Earth.

Similarly for his other shipmates. But they did all possess an advantage over him. They were older, and had backgrounds to come home to. There were even a couple of marriages that had withstood so long a separation. Peter Koskinen had nobody. The fallout during the war missed the tiny resort town in northern Minnesota where he was a child, but the subsequent epidemics did not. The Institute picked the eight-year-old survivor out of an orphanage and raised him with several thousand others who scored equally well on IQ. It was rough. Not that the school was harsh—they did their best to supply parental surrogates—but the country needed a lot of trained minds and needed them in one tearing hurry. Koskinen took a master's degree in physics with a minor in symbolics at the age of eighteen. That same year the Astronautics Authority accepted his application for the ninth Mars expedition, the one which would stay long enough to learn something about the Martians, and he shipped out.

He straightened. *I refuse to feel sorry for myself,* he decided. *I am twenty-three years old, in excellent health, with a substantial bank account. In a few more days, when I make my official report to the board, I'm going to blow the lid off space technology and get myself a niche in the history books. Meanwhile nothing ails me except that I'm not used to Earth yet. You can't spend some of your most impressionable years on another world, so different it's like a dream, and instantly become just like six billion Earthlings.*

"Got to start sometime, lad," he said half aloud, and went into the bath cubby to check his appearance. The high-collared red blouse, flowing blue pants and soft shoes he had bought today were, he had been assured, in fashion. He wondered whether to depple his short blond beard, but decided not to: he was rather baby-faced without it, snub nose, high cheekbones, oblique blue eyes. His body was muscular; Captain Twain had insisted the gang exercise regularly, and lugging a hundred Earth-pounds of survival equipment around was no picnic either. Koskinen had been surprised at how readily he re-adapted to home gravity. The thick, dusty, humid air and late summer temperature were harder on him than weight.

I guess I'll do, he told himself anxiously, and started toward the main door.

It chimed.

For a startled instant, Koskinen didn't move. Who——? Someone off the ship, he wondered with quick hopefulness, as much at loose ends as himself? He remembered to look at the scanner. But the screen was blank.

Out of order? The chime sounded again. Koskinen pressed the Unlock button.

The door opened and two men stepped in. One of them thumbed the Lock switch as the door closed again. His other hand manipulated a small flat box. The scanner came back to life with a view of an empty glideway outside. The man dropped the jamming box into his blouse pocket. His companion had moved along the wall until he commanded a view of the cubby.

Koskinen stood motionless, bewildered. They were bulky men, he saw, soberly clad, their faces hard but almost without expression. "Hey," he began, "what's this about?" his voice trailed off, as if rubbery floor and soundproof panels absorbed it.

The man by the cubby snapped, "Are you Peter J. Koskinen, from the USAAS *Boas*?"

"Y-yes. But——"

"We're from Military Security." The man pulled forth a wallet and flipped it open. Koskinen looked at the identification card, from the photograph back to the features, and felt his belly tighten.

"What's the matter?" he asked, shakily, for even an innocent fresh off the boat know that MS wasn't called in to solve mere crimes. "I——"

The man put away his wallet. Koskinen had seen the name Sawyer. The one by the door remained anonymous. "Our bureau's gotten a report about you and your work on Mars," Sawyer said. His eyes, bullet-colored, never left Koskinen's. "First tell me, though, you got any appointments tonight? Going to meet anybody?"

"No. No, I——"

"Good. We'll be checking all your statements, remember, by psychointerrogation among other things. Better not lie to us."

Koskinen backed a step. He lifted hands gone wet and cold. "What's the matter?" he whispered. "Am I under arrest? What for?"

"Let's call it protective custody," said Sawyer in a slightly more amiable tone. "Technical arrest, yes, but just a technicality as long as you cooperate."

"But what've I *done*?" Sudden anger jumped up in Koskinen. "You can't quiz me under drugs," he exclaimed. "I know my rights."

"The Supreme Court ruled three years ago, chum, that in cases involving the national security, PI methods are allowable. The evidence can't be used in court—yet. It's only to make sure——" Sawyer almost pounced. "Where's the gizmo?"

"The what?" Koskinen began to tremble.

"The gadget. The shielding machine. You took it off the *Boas* with your luggage. Where is it?"

Pretty nearly was *my luggage*, a distant, crazily humorous part of Koskinen thought. *You don't carry much in the way of personal effects on a spaceship.* "What-what-what do you want with it?" he heard himself stammer. "I never . . . stole. I only wanted it handy for when I . . . make my report——"

"Nobody's called you a thief," said the man by the door. "It simply happens that gadget is important to security. Who else knows about it, besides the other expedition members?"

"No one." Koskinen moistened his lips. The horror began to ebb a little. "I've got it . . . right here. In this room."

"Good. Break it out."

Koskinen stumbled to the cabinet and pressed the button. The wall slid back revealing a few changes of clothes, a rain poncho, and a parcel about three feet by two by one, wrapped in yesterday's picture paper and tied with string. "There," he pointed. His finger shook.

"Is that the whole works?" Sawyer asked suspiciously.

"It's not big. I'll show you." Koskinen squatted to untie the package. Sawyer clapped a hand on his shoulder and pulled him back.

"No you don't! Keep away from that!"

Koskinen tried to swallow the rage that returned in him. He was a free American citizen who had deserved well of his country. Who did these flat-feet think they were?

MS, that's who. The knowledge was chilling.

Not that he had ever had much to do with them before, or had heard them accused of unnecessary ill-usage. But one spoke about them softly.

Sawyer made a quick, expert check around the room. "Nothing else," he nodded. "Okay, Koskinen, check out of here and we'll be on our way."

He started throwing clothes into the suitcase which had also been acquired today. Koskinen went jerkily to the phone, rang the desk, and mumbled about an emergency that forced him to leave. He signed and thumbprinted a check; the clerk recorded a facsimile down below and asked if he wanted a bellboy. "No, thanks." Koskinen switched off and looked into the anonymous agent's face. "How long will I be gone?" he pleaded.

The agent shrugged. "I only work here. Let's go."

Koskinen carried his own bag, Sawyer had the package, the third man stood on the other side with a hand resting nonchalantly in one pocket.

The glideway carried them down the corridor. At the third branch they took an upward belt, straight to the roofport. A young man and a girl descended on the opposite strip. Her tunic was a wisp of iridescence from bosom to knees, her hair was piled high and sprayed with micalite, her laugh seemed to come from across immense distances. Koskinen had not felt so alone since he stood hearing pine trees in the night wind and saw his mother die.

Nonsense, nonsense, he told himself. Everything was under control. That was what the Protectorate was for, to keep things under control, to keep cities from going up in radioactive smoke again, and Military Security was no more than the intelligence agency of the Protectorate. Now that he thought about it, the potential barrier effect did have war-like possibilities. Though not for aggressive war. Or did it? Maybe the Security people—good Lord, perhaps Marcus himself—wanted no more than to be reassured on that point.

Yet he was being hustled along by Sawyer's impatient grip on his elbow, and the other man must have a gun in that pocket, and they were going to take him somewhere, incommunicado, and fill him with mind drugs. . . . Suddenly, blindingly, he wished he were back on Mars.

On the edge of Trivium Charontis, looking across the Elysian desert, where the small brilliant sun spilled light from a sky like purple glass, a universe of light, floored with red and tawny dunes, on to the horizon where a dust storm walked crowned with ice crystals; a stone tower which was old when Earthlings hunted mam-

moths; Elkor's huge form coming from behind, scarcely to be heard rustling in that thin sharp air; the palp laid on Koskinen's neck, so strong he felt the detailed touch through his thermsuit fabric, yet gentle as a woman's hand, and the coded vibrations that could by now be understood as readily as English, sensed through flesh and bone: "Sharer-of-Hopes, there came to me, while I merged myself with the stars last night, a new aspect of reality which may bear on the problem that gives us mutual joy."

Then the three men were stepping from the kiosk onto the roof. An ordinary-looking aircar balanced a little way from those which were simply parked. Sawyer nodded to the attendant who seemed intimidated, and slid back the door. "In," he said. Koskinen entered the plastic teardrop and sat down in the middle of the front seat. The agents flanked him, Sawyer at the manual controls. They fastened their safety belts. The light on the radar post turned green. Sawyer pushed the stick and the car shot upward.

II

THE sun was down and low-level megalopolis was quite dark, strung with electric jewels further than Koskinen could see—from Boston, Massachusetts, to Norfolk, Virginia, he recalled vaguely, and eastward to Pittsburgh, where it extended a tendril to meet the complex derived from Chicago. Skyscrapers and Centers reared above that hazy dusk, their heights still catching daylight. The western sky arched greenish over the sunset embers. He recognized Venus and two crawling sparks that were relay satellites. There were more aircars than he remembered from boyhood, darting on a score of traffic levels. Material prosperity was on the way back at last, he thought. A transcontinental liner slanted huge and silvery across the lanes, bound for Cape Cod seadrome. He watched it with longing.

Sawyer set the autopilot and punched for Washington. The car was assigned a medium level, which it entered when the liner was safely past.

Sawyer took out a pack of cigarettes. "Smoke?" he invited Koskinen.

"No, thanks." With an idiotic need to talk, say anything as long as the humming silence in the vehicle could be held off, he explained, "We couldn't on Mars, you see."

"Oh, yes. When your oxygen had to be recycled——"

"No, weight and space was what ruled out tobacco," Koskinen said. "Oxygen was no problem. Not toward the end, at least. With what we'd learned from the Martians—together with them, I should say—we developed an air reclaimer the size of your fist, with capacity enough for two men at top metabolic rate. I've included one in the shield unit. Naturally, when I was traveling around on the surface of Mars, using the potential field instead of a thermsuit and helmet . . ."

Sawyer stiffened. "Cut that!" he barked. "I shouldn't hear any more."

"But you're Security," Koskinen said in astonishment.

"I'm not the boss man," Sawyer said, "and I don't want them to wipe my brain of what I'm not supposed to know. Too often you lose more memories than they figured on."

"Shut up," said his companion. Sawyer showed a second's alarm, then clamped his lips. Koskinen sagged back. *Would they erase memories in me?* he thought sickly.

The companion turned around and stared through the rear window. "How long's that car been behind us?" he snapped.

Sawyer looked too. Koskinen couldn't help doing the same, though he saw nothing but a vehicle at the standard medium-speed distance, not noticeably different from those which moved parallel on either side. "I dunno," Sawyer said dryly. "We're not the only ones going to Washington."

The other man took a spyscope from the glove compartment and peered through it. "Yeh," he grunted. "Same car as followed us from Jersey. I paid attention."

"There are a lot of blue 2012 Eisenhowers," Sawyer said.

"I noticed the license number too," the other man snorted. "You better go back to the Academy."

"But——" Sweat sprang forth in tiny beads on Sawyer's cheeks.

"Now how much of a coincidence is it that a car which happened to get right at our rear on the way to Philly then happened to leave the traffic pattern when we did, and happened to hang around in the streets for precisely as long as we were in the Hotel Von Braun, and then by sheer chance headed off for Washington at the same moment as us?" The man spoke angrily. "And no closed circuit com in this heap to call HQ! Somebody's head will roll."

"We got our orders in such a hurry," Sawyer argued. "Maybe that's an escort there. Yeah, sure. A shadow wouldn't be that amateurish. HQ doesn't always tell you when you're going to be escorted."

"If there was time to arrange an escort, there was time to find us an armored car with a closed talkie circuit," the other man said. "That guy's a foreigner. What do we do about him?"

Sawyer touched the phone. "Call the regular police," he suggested. "Or HQ itself."

"And let half the continent know something big's going on? Not till the situation gets worse than this." The man leaned over Koskinen and punched the pilot board. The telltale screen lit up with REQUEST MAXIMUM CIVILIAN SPEED FOR THIS ROUTE.

"What's happening?" Koskinen managed to breathe.

"Don't worry, kid," said the agent. "When Control yanks us into the top lane, those birds'll have to wait—about three minutes, I'd guess, at this traffic density—for the next opening. That's thirty miles and a lot of other cars put between us."

"But——but——"

Sawyer had regained composure. "This is the sort of thing we're trying to protect you against," he said, not unkindly. "How long do you think you'd live if the Chinese got their hooks on you?"

"Oh, he might live quite a while," said the other agent, "but he wouldn't enjoy it much. Whoops, here we go!"

Somewhere down in the night, the Control computer identified a break through which a car could safely rise. The warning bell rang and Koskinen was pressed back against his seat cushions. Riding lights were switching on at this twilit moment, so that he fell upward through a sudden blurred galaxy of red and green suns. Then they were beneath him, part of the jewels strung over megalopolis. The overhead canopy showed him a sky still dusky blue, the first stars blinking forth, no trace of man except the satellites and one remote stratoliner.

The car leveled off. "Whew!" Sawyer rubbed the back of a hand across his forehead. "I'm glad to get out of there, I can tell you."

"But what could they have done?" Koskinen blurted. "I mean, under Control——unless they had an illegal override circuit——"

"So do we, except for us it's authorized," the other agent grunted. "I can't see a dogfight down in the crowded lanes, no. Especially since the cops'd be there in two minutes. But those boys aren't playing for candy. There are stunts they could have tried."

Sawyer relaxed a little. "The main drawback to this lane is that we might be stacked up above Washington, waiting for clearance to land, longer than it'd take us to get there at average speed. How about ducking down again pretty soon?"

"Uh-huh. Not that I expect——"

Koskinen, looking at the stars and wondering horribly whether he would see them again, was the first to spy the stratoship. "What's that?" he called. The two agents jumped in their seats.

The craft struck downward, a great black bullet, unlighted, exhaust nearly invisible. Koskinen's ears, used to thin air, heard the wail as it drew close. The car rocked.

"Military!" Sawyer exploded. He flung open a panel and pulled a switch. Override, Koskinen thought wildly; escape from the rigid course and speed set by Control——

The armored hull loomed monstrous in the canopy. The aircar leaned over and powerdived groundward. Traffic scattered on each side as Control tried to compensate. Across delirium Koskinen saw Control's failure. Two pairs of red-and-green lights wobbled together, merged, went out, and a meteor trailed fire and smoke down into darkness.

"Hang on!" the nameless man shouted. "The cops'll be coming!" Then the safety belt dug into Koskinen's stomach. His head, thrown forward, almost struck the instrument board. The crash rattled his teeth.

"Grapple!" he heard Sawyer yell. "They got a satellite recovery grapple on us!" Through the canopy, Koskinen glimpsed lines drawn taut. The car tilted crazily. The fleeting lights fell away again. They were bound up.

Sawyer slammed the phone buttons. There was no response. "They've jammed our transmission," he groaned. He leaned on the main drive switch till the engine roared and vibration nearly shook the car apart. "No use." He cut power and slumped. "We can't bust that mesh. Any chance the cops can intercept?"

"Not yonder," his companion said through clenched jaws. "Even lugging us, it can outrun any police car even built. But if the Air Force gets the word in time to scramble a pursuit squadron, we might get rescued yet."

Through the creakings and shakings, Koskinen began to hear a low whistle. Outside he saw blue-blackness and the sun again on the western horizon. They must be entering the stratosphere.

And a leak had been opened in the abused chassis. He felt his eardrums pop as pressure diminished.

"That car shadowing us did have a closed com circuit," said the unidentified agent slowly. "They were in constant touch with the stratoship. It dawdled at extreme altitude, beyond range of Control's radars. Must've taken off in the first place from somewhere in America, or Continental Defense would've spotted it. That's why they were so obvious about tailing us. They figured we'd do exactly what we did, rise high enough to be snatched from above. So they're Chinese. Nobody else has that kind of organization or that much brains."

Both men had guns in their hands. "Wh-what can we do?" Koskinen faltered. His heart pounded as if to crack his ribs. Breath grew scant; a cold draft struck his ankles.

"Break out the oxygen masks and fight," Sawyer said. "We've still got a chance. Having us hanging in a grapple net from their belly slows 'em down. The cops must already have alerted MS. Con Defense radar's going to lock onto them inside of ten minutes. A pursuit squadron will overhaul 'em in ten minutes more."

"They must realize that too," said the other man. His eyes never left the canopy, where the whale shape gleamed through the mesh, edged with night and stars.

The car jerked. A square of deeper blackness opened in the hull above——no, there were lights——"They're taking us aboard!" Sawyer gasped.

His companion sat rigid, hardly seeming alive

except for the blood that trickled from his nose. "Yeah," he said. "I was afraid of that."

His gun swung about. Koskinen looked down the muzzle. "I'm sorry, kid," the agent murmured.

"What do you mean?" a stranger cried through Koskinen's head.

"We can't let them have you. Not if you're as important as I gather you are."

"No!"

"Goodbye, kid."

It was not Koskinen's will which responded. That would have been too slow. But he had practiced judo on Mars for fun and exercise. The animal in him took over the learned reflexes.

He had twisted around in the seat to face the agent. His left hand batted out, knocked the gun aside. It went off with a hiss, startlingly loud beside Koskinen's ear. His right fist was already rocketing upward. It struck beneath the nose. The agent's face seemed to disintegrate.

Koskinen snapped his skull backward. It banged against Sawyer's chin. The man barked. Koskinen reached over his shoulder, got Sawyer by the neck, and hauled the agent's larynx across his own collarbone. He bore down, brutally. Already oxygen-starved, Sawyer made a choking noise and went limp.

Koskinen sagged. Blackness whirled and buzzed around him. A quiver through the car stabbed awareness back into his brain. The hatch was just above the canopy now, like an open mouth. He glimpsed a man on the edge of it, thermsuited, air-helmeted, and armed with a rifle. The car would be in the ship's hold in one more minute. Then, unencumbered, the ship would have a chance of escaping to wherever it had come from.

Sawyer and the other agent stirred. For a fractional second, Koskinen thought: *My God, what am I doing? I attacked two MS men . . . I'm leaving them here to be captured——*

But they meant to kill me. And I haven't time to help them.

He had already somehow unbuckled his safety belt. He scrambled over the seatback. The parcel lay on the rear seat. He snatched it. His free hand fumbled with the door catch. The sound of air, whistling from the interior toward stratospheric thinness, filled his universe.

The car bumped over the hatch frame. Koskinen got the door unlocked. Swords rammed through his eardrums as he encountered the full pressure differential. The thermsuited man aimed the rifle at him.

He jumped from the open door, out through the hatch, and started falling.

First you protect your eyeballs. They can freeze.

Koskinen buried his face in the crook of his left arm. Darkness enclosed him, weightlessness and savage cold. His head whirled with pain and roarings. The last lean breath he had drawn in the car was still in his lungs, but clamoring to get out. If he gave way to that pressure, reflex would make him breathe in again. And there wasn't much air at this height, but there was enough that its chill would sear his pulmonary system.

Blind, awkward with a hand and a half available to him, aided only by a little space experience with free fall—very little, since the *Franz Boas* made the crossing at one-fourth gee of nuclear-powered acceleration—he tore the paper off his shield unit. He and it would have different terminal velocities, but as yet there was so tenuous an atmosphere that everything fell at the same rate. He fumbled the thing to him. Now . . . where was that right shoulder strap? The unit was adjusted incorrectly, and he couldn't make readjustments while tumbling through heaven. . . . Panic snatched at him. He fought it down with a remnant of consciousness and went on groping.

There!

He slipped his arm through, put his head over against that biceps, and got his left arm into the opposite loop. The control panel flopped naturally across his chest. He felt about with fingers gone insensible until he found the master switch, and threw it. In one great gasp he breathed out and opened his eyes.

Cold smote like a knife.

He would have screamed, but his lungs were empty and he had just enough sense left not to try filling them. *Too high yet, too high*, he thought in his own disintegration. *Got to get further down. How long? Square root of twice the distance divided by gee——Gee, Elkor, I miss you. Sharer-of-Hopes, when you sink your personality into the stars these nights do you include the blue star Earth? No, it's winter now in your hemisphere, you're adream, hibernation, hiber, hyper, hyperspace, is the shield really a section of space folded through four extra dimensions, dimens, dim, dimmer, OUT!*

At the last moment of consciousness, he turned off the unit.

He was too numb to feel if there was any warmth around him. But there must be, for he could breathe again. Luckily his attitude wasn't prone, or the air-stream pounding into his open mouth could have done real damage. He sucked greedily, several breaths, before he remembered to turn the field back on.

Then he had a short interval in which to fall. He saw the night sky above him, not the loneliness and the wintry stars of the stratosphere, which reminded him so much of Mars, but Earth's wan sparks crisscrossed by aircar lights. The sky of the eastern American megalopolis, at least; that lay below him still, though he had no idea what archaic city boundaries he had crossed. He didn't see the stratoship. Well, naturally. He'd taken the crew by surprise when he jumped, and by the time they reacted he was already too far down for them to dare give chase.

Suddenly he realized what he hadn't stopped to think before——he *was* over a densely populated area. At his speed he was a bomb. *God*, he cried wildly, *or Existence, or whatever you are, don't let me kill anyone!*

The city rushed at him. It swallowed his view field. He struck.

To him it was like diving into thick tar. The potential barrier made a hollow shell around his body, and impact flung him forward with normal, shattering acceleration until he encountered that shell. Momentum carried him a fractional inch into it. Then his kinetic energy was absorbed, taken up by the field itself and shunted to the power pack. As for the noise, none could penetrate the shield. He rebounded very gently, rose to his feet, shaky-kneed, stared into a cloud of dust and heard his own harsh breath and heartbeat.

The dust settled. He sobbed with relief. He'd hit a street—hadn't even clipped a building. There were no red human fragments around, only a crater in the pavement from which cracks radiated to the sidewalks. Fluoro lamps, set far apart, cast a dull glow on brick walls and unlighted windows. A neon sign above a black, shut doorway spelled UNCLE'S PAWN SHOP.

"I got away," Koskinen said aloud, hardly daring to believe. His voice wobbled. "I'm free. I'm alive."

Two men came running around a corner. They were thin and shabbily dressed. Ground-level tenements were inhabited only by the poorest. They halted and gaped at the human figure and the ruined pavement. A bar of purulent light fell across one man's face. He began jabbering and gesturing, unheard by Koskinen.

I must have made one bong of a racket when I hit. Now what do I do?

Get out of here. Till I've had a chance to think!

He switched off the field. His first sensation was warmth. The air he had been breathing was what he had trapped at something like 20,000 feet. This was thick and dirty. A sinus pain jabbed through his head; he swallowed hard to equalize pressures. Sound engulfed him—machines pounding somewhere, a throb underfoot, the enormous rumble as a train went by not far away, the two men's shouts, "Hey, what the devil, who the devil're you——?"

A woman's voice joined theirs. Koskinen spun and saw more slum dwellers pouring from alleys and doorways. A dozen, two dozen, excited, noisy, gleeful at any excitement in their gray lives. And he must be something to see, Koskinen realized. Not only because he'd come down hard enough to smash concrete. But he was in good, new, upper-level clothes. On his back he carried a lumpy metal cylinder; the harness included a plastic panel across his chest, with switches, knobs, and three meters. Like some science fiction hero on the 3D. For a second he wondered if he could get away with telling them a film was being shot, special effects and——No. He began to run.

Someone clutched at him. He dodged and fled past the crowd. A halloo rose from them. The shield unit dragged at his shoulders; ten pounds added up like fury when you were exhausted. He threw a glance behind. The street lamps marched in an endless double row, skeleton giants with burning heads, but so far apart that darkness welled around each one. The walls rose sheer on either side. A network of tubeways, freight belts, power lines shut out the sky above, except for a red glow. A train screeched around some corner. He could just see the men who pursued, just hear their yelps.

He pressed elbows against ribs and settled down to running. Surely he was in better shape than these starvelings. And with more to hope for, which also counted. What did they have to look forward to, when machines crowded them from their last jobs and population growth outpaced welfare services? A man couldn't fight, or even run very well, when the heart had been eroded out of him. Could he?

The street, intended for trucks, came to an intersection and looped above a monorail track. Koskinen heard a nearing wail in the iron. He sprinted into the shadow of the overpass, dodged among its pillars. The train came into sight and bore down on him behind a blinding headlamp. Koskinen sprang, stumbled on the rail, picked himself up, and got across an instant before the locomotive went by. It shook his bones with noise. Dust swirled grittily into his nostrils. He hugged a wall and remembered that he could have made himself invulnerable by throwing the shield switch. But then he'd be immobile too, unless the train knocked him aside. . . . It brawled on past. Behind the freight cars came the passenger section, sallow people glimpsed through dirty windows.

But I meant to break my trail. I've got to be out of view before the train is by me. Koskinen groped his way along the wall. The oily wind of the train's passage buffeted him. He bumped into another column supporting the overpass and fumbled his way back onto the street. Quickly then he ran down its emptiness until an alley yawned on his left. He ducked into that.

The train vanished. He crouched in darkness, but no mob came after him. Not seeing him, they must have given up. Their chase had been mostly from curiosity anyhow.

The alley opened on a courtyard enclosed by four crumbling tenements. Koskinen paused in its shadows to pant. Since there was nothing above the house roofs here except some power lines, he could see the sky—red haze, no stars—and the beautiful, arrogant heights of a Center, half a mile or so away, looming over these mean walls. Traffic hummed and rumbled everywhere around, but no life was to be seen except for one gaunt cat.

Wonder where I am? Could be anywhere be-

tween Boston and Washington, I suppose, depending on which direction the stratoship took while it had us netted. Koskinen forced his pulse and respiration down toward normal. His legs were weak but his mind was clearing. This must be a bomb-drop district, hastily rebuilt after the war and never improved since, except for the Centers; and they were towns to themselves, of course, where nobody could afford to live who didn't have the skills that an automation economy demanded. The deduction wasn't much help; there were a lot of bombsites.

What to do?

Call the police? But the police would get an alert about him from Military Security. And the MS men had tried to kill him.

Cold settled back into Koskinen. The fact couldn't be, he told himself frantically. Not in the United States of America! The country which mounted guard on a sullen world—self-appointed guardian at that; but who else could handle the job?—must be tough. Of course. But it didn't use agents who were murderers!

Or did it? Perhaps the emergency had been precisely that great. Perhaps, in some way he couldn't guess, the survival of the United States depended on Peter Koskinen's not falling into foreign hands. If so, he need only report to MS. They'd apologize for everything, and give him the best of care, and release him when——

Well, when?

Dad and Mother are dead, he choked, *and Mars is lost behind this filthy sky. Who have I got?*

He remembered Dave Abrams. It was like a

thawing in him. Dave had been his closest buddy. Still was, by Existence. And a levelheaded chap. And Dave's father was on the board of directors of General Atomics, which meant influence comparable to a U.S. Senator's. Yes, that was the drill. Call Dave. Arrange a meeting somewhere. Work out what to do, and then do it, with powerful friends at his back.

Returning nerve brought Koskinen a consciousness of how hungry he was. And thirsty. As thirsty as the time his air humidifier failed on the expedition along Cerberus Canal . . . the time he and Elkor traveled to the Philosophers, whose very shape he could no longer quite recall. . . . That had been in the second Earth-year, hadn't it? Yes. The third year they'd achieved their breakthrough, as Martian and Terrestrial science viewpoints, ways of thinking, fused into a concept of energy phenomena that was new to both planets. In the fourth year they worked out the engineering practice and built portable potential-barrier units for everyone on the *Boas*. But only this one had been brought home, what with weight restrictions and—— Koskinen realized he was maundering. Lightheaded. Let's find an eatery. Praise luck, he had a well-filled wallet in his pants.

IV

CROSSING the courtyard, he emerged on a more or less residential street. The neglected paving showed that few industrial vehicles used it. Brick and concrete buildings were jammed together, boxlike, none more than five stories high. A good many people were out on their balconies for a breath of air. Others drifted along the sidewalks: old shuffling men, tough-looking boys with hoods pulled over their brows and cigarettes in their mouths, a gaggle of adolescent girls in sleazy ultrafashions that would have been more interesting if their figures had had a few more years to develop, a weary mother hauling a whining small fry home from a game in the street. More could be seen through their apartment windows, staring at the inevitable 3D screens.

Koskinen walked rapidly, making himself ignore the looks and mutters. A place to eat, a place to eat. . . . Around the next corner the local supermarket flashed neon at him.

Few were inside at this hour. He noticed how

27

run-down and untidy the establishment was, but the prices marked were cheap . . . yes, didn't the government subsidize low-level stores? Passing Drugs, Clothes, Laundry, and Tools, he saw a sign: RESTAURANT—animated, a girl dressed in an apron, tossing flapjacks—beyond shelves of groceries, and cut through that section. The checkout robot couldn't identify the thing on his back. "One moment, please," said the tape. A buzzer sounded, a scanner lit up, and a human voice said from the mike, "Okay, go on. I don't know what you got there, asco, but you didn't shoplift it here."

Koskinen grinned feebly and went on. The eatery wasn't an automat, he discovered with some surprise. Well, a degree of handicraft survived on the very poorest levels, where any pay was better than none—and among the wealthy, who could afford live service. A large man with sad eyes stood behind the counter; his belly sagged against it. Two other men nursed coffee cups at the farther end. They lacked even the nominal grooming of local residents; their blouses were stained and greasy, they hadn't shaved for a week. The big one watched the 3D in the corner, some idiotic story about a war-time mission across Australia. The other sat with a cigarette between his fingers and stared at a private dream.

"What'll you have?" The sad man touched a button and today's menu appeared on a screen. Koskinen had visioned a huge rare steak with French fried onions. But what low-level joint would carry actual meat? He settled for a goomburger and alga stew. "And your biggest bottle of beer to start with," he added.

"Spiked?" asked the counterman.

"Hm?" Koskinen looked, puzzled, into the heavy face. "You mean vodka added?"

"What you talking about? I mean buzz juice. Mescalinoid, skizzo, neoin, or what do you want?"

"Uh, nothing. Just plain beer. I need a clear head tonight."

"Mmm . . . yeah. You're from topside, aren'tcha? Fancy clothes and a suntan. You'd better not get too happy at that, around here." The counterman took a liter of Raketenbräu from the cooler, opened it and set it before Koskinen. "In fact," he said, "my advice to you is, catch the first train back. Or better yet, phone for a taxi to come and fly you home."

Koskinen's fingers clenched on the bottle. "Is this such a bad district?" he asked slowly.

"N-no. Not us natives, except for the boy packs. But we're not far from the Crater, and a lot of their people come over this way." The man made a furtive gesture toward the two who sat at the other end. The one who was not smoking had turned small eyes in a slashed and broken face away from the 3D and was looking openly, insolently, at the newcomer.

The counterman pushed a not very clean glass toward Koskinen. He used the opportunity to whisper: "We got guards in here, so we don't get any rough stuff. But you better not go out alone in the street. He guesses you've got money on you."

Koskinen shrugged. There was no reason why he should not leave by taxi. "Thanks for the warning," he said. He slipped the shield unit off his back and laid it under his stool.

"What is that thing, anyway?" asked the counterman aloud.

"Experimental," Koskinen said. The question was not pursued; people didn't get nosy on low-level. Koskinen drank deep. The cool taste tingled the whole way down. He attacked the food ravenously. Confidence flowed into him.

The man who had been watching him left the counter and went to a phone booth. Whoever he called didn't choose to transmit a picture. The man switched off and went back to his seat, where he joggled the dreamer awake. They muttered to each other. Koskinen paid no attention. He finished his meal and walked past them to the phone. Gifted with a good memory, he punched out the number Abrams had given him. The screen flashed: PLEASE DEPOSIT ONE DOLLAR FOR THREE MINUTES, TWO DOLLARS FOR VISUAL.

Why . . . that was the charge for a local call, wasn't it? Koskinen dropped in two coins and leaned out of the booth. "Hey," he called, "where am I, anyway?"

"Huh?" said the counterman.

"I'm, uh, I'm lost. What section is this?"

"Bronx." The counterman rolled his eyes toward the ceiling. The two others grinned. Koskinen closed the door as the screen came to life. He was too nervous to sit down and threw a hasty glance at the telltale. But it wasn't glowing; no tape was being made at the other end of the line.

A plump, aging woman looked out at him. Her eyes were red-rimmed and she twisted a wedding ring around and around on her finger. "Is this Mrs. Abrams?" Koskinen asked. She nodded mutely. "May I speak to your son David, please?"

"He isn't here." Her voice was almost inaudible.

Oh no! "Do you know where I can get in touch with him? It's pretty urgent."

"No . . . no . . . who are you?"

"Pete Koskinen. Dave's shipmate——"

She jerked as if burned. "I don't know you!" she gasped. "I don't know anything about you."

"But——ma'am——" Koskinen's spine crawled. He forced calmness into his tone. "Is something wrong? Dave must have mentioned me. If you don't know where he is now, could you have him call me back?" He stopped and thought. "That is, I'll find a hotel room, then call and give you my number and——"

"No!" she screamed. "They arrested him! Don't you know they came and took him away?"

Koskinen stood unmoving.

She seemed to realize she had said too much. "You'd better get in touch with the police yourself," she chattered. "There's some awful misunderstanding, I'm certain it's a misunderstanding. Maybe you can help clear it up. Davy's father has been on the phone for hours, ever since——

Calling everybody. Even people in Congress. But he can't learn a thing. Maybe you can help——" she began to cry.

Is her line tapped? Koskinen shoved down the switch.

Briefly, he wanted to run. But that was senseless. He had no place to go. If a director of General Atomics couldn't spring his own son, what use—— *I'll have one more try. Captain Twain himself.*

The skipper had gone to his home town in Oregon, Koskinen knew, even though he hadn't any close relatives left there. Koskinen dialled Information. "Please be patient, sir," the computer tech said. "A one-minute line break is due shortly."

What the devil? Oh, yes. The shifting configuration of the radio relay satellites. "I'll wait," Koskinen said.

"If your party isn't at home, do you wish a special search made?"

"Uh, no. Just find me where he's staying. I'll talk to anybody."

The screen blanked. Koskinen stood alone with the soft, silly "interlude music." He shifted from foot to foot, tugged his beard, hammered a fist into the other palm. Sweat trickled along his ribs.

There was a rap on the door. Koskinen turned about with an oath. The bristle-chinned man who had made the previous call stood outside. Koskinen flung the door open in a surge of belligerence. "Well?" he barked.

"Ya gonna be through soon, asco?" The tone

was not impolite, but burly shoulders were hunched.

"A few minutes yet. There should be other phones in this place, if you're in a hurry."

"Nah, nah, that's okay. I was just wondering, sort of. We don't get many topsiders down here. I was wondering if you was looking for a little fun, maybe." The damaged face attempted a leer.

"No, thanks."

"I know some good places. Better'n anything yuh find topside."

"No! I'm going to finish my call and get the devil out of here. Okay by you?"

Momentarily the man glared. Smoothing his expression, he nodded. "Don't getcha guts hot. I was just try'n'a be frien'ly." Koskinen closed the door. The other went back to the counter and spoke to his companion. Both looked pleased, Koskinen thought.

Some enormous time later, the phone buzzed. Koskinen whirled around so fast he bumped his knee on the seat. The pain stung him into a little more self-control. "We have your number, sir," a human operator said. "In Eugene, Oregon." He dropped in the required number of buck pieces.

The screen showed him a strange man's face. "Is Captain Silas Twain there?" Koskinen asked.

"Who wants to know?" said the other. His manner was hard and wary.

Koskinen bristled. "Who do you think you are?"

The man paused, reached a decision, and said: "Military Security. Captain Twain has been killed resisting a kidnap attempt. Who are you?''

Koskinen shook his head, trying to clear the darkness out. "Is that the truth?" he mumbled. "Or another story?"

"Ask the news service. Now, who are you? Quick!"

"Just . . . an old friend. J-J-Jim Longworth," Koskinen stammered, fishing a classmate's name from an impossibly remote past. "I heard the Mars expedition was back and——I thought——" Because the agent looked satisfied, he switched off.

Wildly, he stared out the booth. The big fellow who had spoken to him was now addressing the counterman. His mouth was drawn into an ugly grimace. The counterman flinched, shivered, nodded again and again, and tottered to the opposite end of the bar where he got furiously busy. The big man went out. The skinny one with the cigarettes remained, not smoking now, alert. It didn't register particularly on Koskinen.

Twain dead. Great, ruddy, unbendable Si Twain, a corpse. But such things didn't happen!

Had MS killed him themselves?

Koskinen slapped the switch up, punched for News, and fed coins into the slot. He scarcely saw or heard the answer girl. "Gimme the latest story on Captain Twain," he almost shrieked, hanging onto the seatback. "Mars expedition. They say he's dead tonight."

"Yes, sir. That story came in only half an hour ago, I remember." The girl punched buttons. A tape began to run, showing a man who said:

"World News Service, Eugene, Oregon, September 12.—— Captain Silas G. Twain, 44, leader of the most recent expedition to Mars, was found murdered in his hotel room today. The body was discovered about 1630 Pacific Daylight Saving Time by Dorinda Joye, 22, a secretary from an agency he had called not long before. There were many signs of a struggle. Beside Captain Twain's body, which had been shot, was that of a man believed to be Chinese. His skull was crushed by a heavy ashtray still in Twain's hand. Police theorized that several intruders had come in the tenth-floor window from an airlift platform and tried to kidnap the spaceman. While resisting he killed one of them. Unable to cope with him and fearing discovery, the others shot him and fled, Police Inspector John Flying Eagle said. The time of Twain's call to Miss Joye's agency fixed the hour of death as no earlier than 1600. Military Security agents moved promptly to occupy the scene and no further comment is being made by any official source.

"The reason for the tragedy remains mysterious. Captain Twain was——"

The commentary went into a hastily assembled orbit, with film clips. Koskinen switched off. Forget that.

Forget MS, and the Chinese, and every other murdering—— His eyes stung. *I'm about to cry*, he thought in a dim surprise.

No use calling anyone else from the ship. I must be the only one still alive and at large, and that's only because I had the shield machine. Let's get out of here before I'm caught too.

Out? Where? I don't know. Right now I don't give a hoot. Just out.

Clumsily, because he trembled and didn't see very well, he punched for a taxi. "Yes, the Old Prole Supermarket. How should I know the address? You've got a directory, haven't you? Use it, for God's sake!" he snapped the switch viciously and stumbled from the booth.

The counterman shrank from him. Terror lay in the sallow features. Koskinen paid small heed. He hoisted the shield generator onto his back and went from the restaurant area.

A stocky man with a gun at his hip stopped him between grocery shelves. " 'Scuse, mister," he said. "I'm a guard. Been watching you on the monitor. You know that bum who talked to you while you were phoning?"

"No," said Koskinen vaguely. "Let me by."

"Him and that other character, they're from the Crater. I've seen 'em around before. So they're up to no good. I don't like the way he talked to Gus at the bar. Plain as day, he told Gus not to warn you about nothing. And then he left his pal and went on out himself."

The dreamy man drifted down another aisle, toward the door. The guard glowered after him. "I can't do nothing till they start acting roochy," he said. "But if I was you, mister, I'd stay here and let me call the cops. You might want an escort home."

Koskinen started. "Police?" MS? "Thanks, no!"

The guard squinted. "You on the lam yourself,

son? You don't look the sort. What's that thing you're wearing?"

"None of your business!" Koskinen snapped. He took off, nearly running. The guard stared a moment, then shrugged.

As the main door opened for him, Koskinen stopped. The truck lot outside was bare and dimly lit. Traffic growled, but not where he could see any. *I better stay inside till the taxi comes*, he thought.

And then where to? A hotel, probably. Not so cheap it was a robbers' den, not so good it would attract MS investigators. Or Chinese, he thought with a shudder. A middle-class, traveling salesman sort of place. He couldn't stay there long, he was too conspicuous. But he could buy a happy pill, get a night's sleep—he was near falling over from weariness—and decide on his next move tomorrow.

A battered green teardrop rolled into the lot. The driver got out. He wore a steel helmet and an anesthetic needle gun, but his vehicle bore the legend COMETEER TAXICAB COMPANY. He strode briskly to the doorway. "You the party wanted a hack?"

"Yes." Koskinen followed him out. He opened the rear door with an unexpected flourish. Koskinen climbed in.

The door slammed on him. One powerful hand took his left wrist and twisted it agonizingly past the shoulder blades. Another arm closed around his throat. "Don't move none and you won't get hurt," said the voice of the man who had talked to him at the booth.

The driver chuckled and got into the front seat. He punched for air clearance and the taxi purred skyward. Koskinen fought to breathe.

Fool, he told himself bitterly. Utter, total, thumblefumb idiot! The men at the counter had planned this from the minute they saw him. They'd called their confederate, on the reasonable guess that Koskinen would want to leave in a taxi. The conversation with him had confirmed that. The confederate had parked around the corner till the big man, the mugger, appeared and told him, "Push it, now; pick 'im up before the real cab gets here." The little smoker had kept an eye on Koskinen till the last moment, ready to dash out and warn the others if anything went wrong. But nothing had. He, Peter Koskinen, was caught.

"That's right," said the mugger. He laughed. "Just relax and enjoy it. We'll letcha off in a mile or so. Reach around with yuh right hand and toss yuh wallet on the floor."

Koskinen obeyed. *But I'm crippled now!* he thought. *I doubt if I've got twenty dollars in change. I daren't call my bank——*

"Okay," grunted the mugger. "He's been good, Tim. So land him near enough to a tube station he'll have a chance uh making it alive."

"X," said the driver, and punched again. Control lowered the taxi to street level and released it. They rolled to a halt between two sheer walls, automated plants no doubt, roofed by a rumbling freight belt. The gloom was thick here.

"Oh, yeh," said the mugger. "Yuh gimmick too. That thing on yuh back—boy, did it ever get in my way just now!—I want that too. Dunno

38

what it is, but mebbe Zigger will, or his girl. Wanna tell me yuhself?''

"No——please——" Koskinen croaked through the pressure.

"Suit yuhself. But get outta them straps. Pronto!"

The stranglehold was released so he could wriggle from the harness. The driver turned around and aimed the needle gun at him. Its metal gleam was barely discernible. "No tricks, now," he said genially.

What have I got to lose?

Koskinen slipped off his shoes, unnoticed in the murk. His hands pretended to tug at his shoulder straps. Groping, he felt the wallet through his socks, and picked it up between both feet.

"Snap along there," said the mugger impatiently.

Koskinen threw the shield switch.

The expanding cylindroidal force shell pushed him off the seat until he occupied midair in a corner. The bandit was shoved against the opposite wall. He must have roared, and perhaps the driver cursed, but they were mere shadows now, altogether silent.

Koskinen put the wallet into his pocket and waited, shaking with reaction. He had become invulnerable to anything they had. Not even gas could penetrate the invisible barrier; and the air cycler guaranteed him oxygen. He saw fists batter. A needle broke on the shield, and the mugger opened his window to let the volatile anesthetic out.

"That's right," Koskinen babbled, crazily,

since they couldn't hear him either. "You can't linger here. There are police cars on patrol, you know. You can't get at me. Shove me out the door and scram! You're whipped. Get rid of me!"

The big man felt around, defining for himself the volume of impenetrability. He threw his shoulder against Koskinen and found that the shell, with its contents, was easily movable; for it added no weight, and energy absorption provided a pseudo-friction. "Push me out and be done, you muckhead!" Koskinen shouted.

The two shadows conferred. The driver bent back to his controls. The taxi sprang into the air.

Great Existence, Koskinen thought. The knowledge clubbed him. *They're taking me along!*

There was sufficient light in the traffic lanes, diffused from below by the dirty air, that he could clearly see the mugger. The big man crouched against the farther wall, his gaze never leaving Koskinen. He had the driver's gun in one hand and a vibro shiv in the other. His eyes were rimmed with white, his chest rose and fell, sweat glistened on his skin. But these bandits had guts, Koskinen knew—the courage to take this fearful thing where it could be studied and perhaps acquired.

What to do?

He could switch off the field long enough to open the door and jump . . . no. That would take a second, at least. A needle would need much less time to cross the car and knock him unconscious.

He could open his defenses and surrender.

No. Not yet. He could always do that, if things got desperate. Let him try to wait out their attempts. Maybe he could even bargain. Maybe, maybe—— His strength collapsed. Folding himself as nearly into a sitting position as the shell allowed, he waited dully for whatever was going to happen.

V

IT wasn't far to the Crater. The taxi left the Control beam and slanted down on manual. Koskinen saw a circle of darkness, below and ahead, carved from the wan light-haze and street-web of the surrounding slum. He could make out a few buildings silhouetted on the rim, one or two windows aglow but otherwise black. Several miles away rose the Center he had seen while on foot, tier after tier climbing zenithward like a luminous fountain; and a couple of skyscrapers were also visible, where worldwide enterprises found housing. He could even see the firefly traffic stream yonder. It might as well all have been on another planet.

Not Mars, though, he thought in his despair. Mars had killed men too: with unbreathable ghostly atmosphere, hunger and thirst and cold and strangeness. But beauty had abided in those deserts, moving forests, stark mesas—and foremost in the great serene Martian minds, which had joined with humans to follow knowledge. *I used to get homesick out there for Earth. For what I missed, now that I think about it, was stuff like green grass and trees, sunlight on my bare skin, wind ruffling a lake, Indian summer, snow, and the people who belonged to such country, the people I knew as a kid. This isn't Earth. Wish me back to our Mars, Sharer-of-Hopes.*

The taxi hovered near the unlit circle while the driver used his phone. Identifying himself? Rumor said that the more powerful chieftains in such places had means to shoot down intruders. Koskinen didn't know. Few upper-level civilians had any real information about the Craters. Koskinen knew only that during the initial postwar reconstruction there'd been too much radioactivity at the bombsites for habitation. As it diminished, the poorest elements of society moved near because such land was cheap or even free. The hardiest went into the craters themselves, finding hideouts where they recruited their strength and from which, in time, they exacted tribute from the low-level dwellers of entire cities. The police, who had enough to do elsewhere, seldom interfered unless things got completely flagrant, and sometimes not then. Any social order was better than none, and the crater barons did impose a structure of sorts on the slums.

The driver switched off. A radio telltale glowed on his panel. He followed the beacon to a landing. Several shadowy forms closed in. The driver emerged and talked for a while. They opened the door and wrestled Koskinen out.

He looked around. They were on a small concrete structure which jutted from the crater bowl about halfway between the rim and the invisible bottom. Its flat roof made a landing platform. Gloom sloped upward on every side, with the faintest vitrification shimmer, until it ended where a series of watch-towers squatted against the surly red haze. A glowlamp in one man's hand revealed half a dozen hard faces, helmeted heads and leather-like jackets, gun barrels aimed inward at the stranger. Two picked Koskinen up and bore him along; the others fanned out on guard. The mugger and the taxi driver went on ahead, while someone else was deputed to flit the vehicle away.

Koskinen lay passive in his shell, aching with tiredness. They carried him through a door at the bottom of the structure, down a ramp, and so into a plastic-lined, fluoro-lit tunnel. A flatbed gocart stood there, onto which his escort got with him. It drove rapidly downward. Before many minutes the passage opened into a much larger tunnel, perhaps a subway which had survived the bomb blast and afterward had been refitted. They must have their own power system here, Koskinen thought, ventilation, heating, every necessity—including, no doubt, food and ammunition for a long siege. The gocart passed others, mostly carrying hired workmen who bobbed their heads respectfully to the warriors. It passed steel doors where machine gun emplacements were built into the walls, and finally stopped at an even more heavily fortified checkpoint. From there the party took a side passage, on foot.

But this was astonishing: a glideway hall, as elegantly decorated as the Von Braun's had been. An open door revealed a suite of darkly shining luxury and taste. Beyond, an intersecting corridor led them past less elaborate but perfectly adequate living quarters, then by a sprawling machine shop and a closed door on which was lettered ELEC-TRONICS—and eventually through a thick double portal into a concrete-block room where the guards set Koskinen down.

He got to his feet. That took a little doing; he must move his center of gravity about until he tilted the rigid force shell onto its broad flat "base." Glancing around, he saw the guardsmen place themselves along the walls, guns trained on him. A workbench held standard laboratory apparatus. Nearby were a telephone and the armored pickup of a monitor screen. *This is where they test anything dangerous*, he decided.

After what seemed a long time, the inner door opened again and let two people in. The guardsmen nodded in salute. Koskinen forced down the exhaustion that made his brain seem full of sand and looked closely at the newcomers.

The man was big, middle-aged, with a kettle belly and a bald pate. He scarcely even had eyebrows. His face was pink and jowly, a blob of a nose, a gash of a mouth. But he moved with a briskness that bespoke muscles. He was gorgeously clad in iridescent blue; rings glittered on his fingers. The spitgun at his hip looked well-worn.

The woman was pleasanter to watch. She was about thirty, Koskinen guessed, tall, a splendid figure and a supple gait. Blue-black hair fell almost to her shoulders. Her face was squarish, with lustrous brown eyes, broad nose, full and sullenly curved lips. Her complexion was a *café-au-lait* that made everyone else look bleached; the white lab coat she wore above an expensive red tunic heightened the effect.

Okay, Koşkinen thought with a prickle along his scalp, *here's the boss in person. What'd the kidnappers call him, Zigger?*

The man walked slowly around him, felt the outlines of the field, pushed him over and studied how he fell and how he regained his feet. Waving his underlings out of ricochet range, he fired a few bullets and watched them drop straight down from the point where they struck. The woman leaned against the workbench and regarded the performance without stirring. At the end, she picked a notepad from among the apparatus, scribbled, and held the page before Koskinen's eyes.

He read, in an unexpected copperplate: "This looks like something we need. Are you interested in selling?"

He shook his head. "Let me go!" he cried.

She frowned and wrote for him: "Make letters with your fingers. Deaf and dumb alphabet. So." She illustrated a few.

Deaf and dumb——? Oh, yes, such tricks doubtless did survive among those who couldn't afford neuroprosthesis. Koskinen spelled out awkwardly: "You cannot get at me and the police are looking for me. Better let me go."

The woman conferred with Zigger. He seemed shaken. She told him something that surprised him, but he gave orders to a guard, who went out. The woman wrote for Koskinen:

"Obviously you have air renewal in there, but I don't see any other supplies. You could be walled up and left to starve. Better come out and talk to us. Zigger keeps his word—when it's convenient." She threw the boss, who was reading over her shoulder, a feline grin; he reddened but made no comment. "He's a bad man to cross, though."

Br'er Rabbit and the brier patch! Koskinen thought in a leap of excitement. "Please do not brick me in," he spelled on his fingers. *If they do, I can expand the field and break down any masonry they can erect—and maybe escape!*

"Okay. Starving's too slow anyway," the woman answered laconically.

The guard returned with a bulky long-barreled object cradled in his arms. The woman wrote: "Do you recognize this?"

Koskinen shook his head. He couldn't see the thing very well.

"A laser gun. It amplifies radiation by stimulating atoms to re-emit in a highly collimated beam. Call it a heat ray."

Oh, yes, Koskinen thought. The will drained out of him. *I've heard about those.*

"I expect that since your force field or whatever it is lets light go back and forth, it will also let infrared by," wrote the woman. "The first shot will be into your foot."

The guard brought the weapon to bear. Koskinen switched the shield off and fell forward on his hands and knees.

VI

THE phone woke him. He turned over, shoved his head under the pillow, and tried to deny its existence. The phone kept buzzing. Koskinen blinked, mouthed a curse, reached out and switched it on.

A dark woman looked from the screen. He gaped, not easily remembering her or where he was. "Good morning," she said, with a smile that went no deeper than her lips. "Good afternoon, rather. *Late* afternoon. I thought you'd been sacked in long enough."

"Huh?" Slowly, in bits and pieces, recollection came back. He'd nearly fainted after the screen was off. They took the unit from him and led him here and gave him a tranquilizer—— He looked around at a small, not unpleasant room with bath. There was only one door, and no window . . . a ventilator grille . . . yes, he was underground, wasn't he? In Zigger's inverted castle.

"I wan't to talk with you," the woman said. "I've ordered dinner." Her smile widened. "Breakfast, to you. The guard'll come fetch you

48

in fifteen minutes. Up, fellah!''

Koskinen crawled from bed as the screen blanked. His clothes were gone, but a closet wall retracted to show several excellent new outfits. A needle spray forced some of the stiffness from his muscles. There was no logic to the fact that a green blouse and gray slacks should cheer him a little. By the time an armed man opened the door, he was ready and famished.

They took the glideway into the luxury section. He was waved through a door which closed behind him. Across a soft, tinted floor, he looked at a suite of several rooms. Some good pictures hung on the walls. The viewall was playing a color abstraction which was too intellectual for his taste, but he was gladdened to recognize Mozart on the taper. The furnishings were low-legged, Oriental, centered about a pedestal that upheld a lovely piece of uncut Lunar crystal. How much had that cost? he wondered.

The woman sat before a table. A white tunic set off her pale brown skin. She waved a hand with a cigarette in it. The other held a cocktail. "Sit down, Pete." Her voice was husky, with a trace of Southern accent. She was a quadroon, he guessed, and probably part Creole.

"How do you know my name?" he asked. Then: "Oh. Sure. Stupid of me, papers in my wallet."

"And a quick check with the news service," she nodded. "You got a fine welcome home, didn't you?"

He seated himself across the table. A servitor rolled in and asked him what he wanted. He realized that he and the woman were the only humans present—though doubtless the guard waited outside, and there might well be an alarm buzzer or a tattler mike in her massive silver bracelet. "I . . . I don't know," he said. "Uh . . . what was that thing the other day? . . . a Tom Collins."

She grimaced. "You need education, I see. Oh, well, it's your palate. Smoke?"

"No, thanks." He wet his lips. "Wh-wh-what did the news have to say about me?"

"Not one thing," she answered, looking straight into his eyes. "As far as the phone or the picture papers know, you're still relaxing at the Von Braun Hotel in Philly. However, we've not been able to contact any of your shipmates."

"I know," he said bleakly. "I only hope MS has them, alive. The Chinese killed Si Twain, you know."

"What?" She sat upright.

"It was on the news," he faltered. "Last night."

"It wasn't today," she said. "Today's story said he died in an accident and anything you heard about a murder was due to a hysterical——" The sensuous mouth grew as harsh as Zigger's. "What's the truth?"

He summoned defiance. "Why should I tell you?"

Her manner softened again, with the mercurialness that had already bewildered him. "Look, Pete," she said, low and rapidly, "you're caught in something tremendous. I spent the day making empirical tests on that gadget of yours. I know a few things it can do, and that alone is enough to drive Zigger wild. We haven't any mind drugs here, but we do have nerve machines, and even uglier stuff. No—'' she raised a slender hand— ''I'm not threatening you. I wouldn't do such a thing to anybody, for any reason. But Zigger would. I'm warning you, Pete. You've had the course. There's no choice but to level with . . . with me, at least.''

''If I do, what then? MS won't thank me.''

''We can get you away from them, if you really don't think they will forgive you. The Crater does give value for value received, after its own fashion. Okay, what happened to Twain?''

The servitor brought his drink. He snatched it and drank blindly. The account stumbled out of him.

She nodded, carefully, struck a fresh cigarette and puffed for a while with her eyes narrowed in thought. At length: ''Yes, obviously last night's account was the right one, and now MS has clamped a lid on the truth. I begin to see the overall picture. Your expedition innocently brings this thing back from Mars, never dreaming what it implies. The men zoom off to their respective homes. They mention the thing to their friends. MS, which has been keeping tabs on them as it routinely does on everything unusual, gets the word within hours. *They* see the possibilities involved. They've got to lock away this machine and everyone who knows anything about it, at least until they can figure out what to do. So they take most of your shipmates into custody.

''But the Chinese have spies of their own,

agents, sleepers, scattered around the world. Everybody knows that. And . . . the Chinese ring was probably on the *qui vive* about this returning expedition. After all, the previous trips had shown the Martians to have a considerable technology, even if it is utterly unlike anything we've imagined on Earth. The *Boas* might well bring back something revolutionary. Especially since your announced purpose was to make an intensive study of the Martian civilization. The Chinese could have worked agents into strategic positions far in advance. You know, people who became close friends of the spacemen's families, that sort of thing. So they got the word almost as soon as MS did. It became a race to capture expedition members.''

Enfeebled as he was from sleep following total nervous exhaustion, and no food, the liquor hit Koskinen like a fist. "Not much use," he blurted through sudden fog. "I had the only unit on Earth. And the only full knowledge about it. Y' see, I was the one who developed it. With Martian help, certainly. But the other guys, they had their own projects.''

She leaned back on the couch, relaxing like a big cat, giving him only the softest of nudges. "Why didn't MS grab you before anyone else, then?''

"Prob'ly didn't get the full story at once. And maybe had some trouble finding me. I'd said I was going to Minneapolis, but at the last minute changed my mind, thought I'd look over the Atlantic supertown. They came fast, anyhow. With the Chinese on their heels.''

"I take it you were escaping from the Chinese

when our boys came upon you?''

"And MS. Also MS." Koskinen finished his drink. "Tried to kill me, MS did." She opened her eyes wide and let them glow at him. He felt he must make himself clear to her, and went through the story.

"I see," she murmured at the end. "Yes, they're a hard-boiled outfit in their own right. How well I know." She reached across the table and squeezed his hand. "But you need food now."

The servitor brought in soup, rolls, authentic butter. She let him eat a while before she chuckled and said, "By the way, I forgot you still don't know my name. I'm Vivienne Cordeiro."

"Pleased to meet you," he mumbled. As his head cleared and strength returned, so did wariness. He cursed himself for giving away so many potential trump cards. Though he must admit she had helped him understand a situation that had seemed a fever dream. "Are you a physicist?"

"Of sorts," she nodded. "Institute kid like you —according to your news biography. They didn't pick me up, however, till I was fifteen." A darkness flitted across her face. "A good many things had happened before then. But no matter now. I run the technical section here. Crater bosses also need someone who understands things like energetics and information theory."

Koskinen said, "You realize the shield unit is still in an early, experimental stage. You'd need a big laboratory and several years to develop the potentialities. Especially the potentialities that no one has yet guessed."

"True. But Zigger could make excellent use of the thing even as is. Let's talk about it. Not in any detail—I doubt if I could follow the math—but in generalities." Koskinen hesitated. "I already know a good bit," she reminded him.

He sighed. "Okay."

"First, is this a Martian machine?"

"Not exactly. I told you the Martians and—well, I—invented it together. They had the field theory but didn't know much practical solid state physics."

"Hm-hm. That means MS can't simply send a spaceship there and demand the full plans. According to all previous reports, the Martians won't play ball with anyone who isn't *simpático* with the humans they've decided to like; and it's no use trying to pretend you are if you aren't, because they know; and the Russians found out the hard way before the war that they can detonate your atomic weapons in your own magazines. Of course, with the American government having the only spaceships these days, nobody else can get to Mars either. This game will be played out here on Earth.

"So what is your invisible screen? A potential barrier?"

Surprised, he nodded. "How did you guess?"

"Seemed reasonable. A two-way potential barrier, I suppose, analogous to a mountain ridge between the user and the rest of the world. But I've determined myself, today, that it builds from zero to maximum within the space of a few centimeters. Nothing gets through that hasn't the needful energy, sort of like the escape velocity needed to get off a planet. So a bullet which hits the screen can't get through, and falls to the ground. But what happens to the kinetic energy?"

"The field absorbs it," he said, "and stores it in the power pack from which the field is generated in the first place. If a bullet did travel fast enough to penetrate, it'd get back its speed as it passed through the inner half of the barrier. The field would push it, so to speak, drawing energy from the pack to do so. But penetration velocity for the unit I've got, at its present adjustment, is about fifteen miles per second."

She whistled. "Is that the limit?"

"No. You can push the potential barrier as high as you like, until you even exclude electromagnetic radiation. That would take a much larger energy storage capacity, of course. For a given capacity, such as my unit has, you can expand the surface of the barrier at the price of lowering its height. For instance, you could enclose an entire house in a sphere centered on my unit, but penetration velocity would be correspondingly less—maybe only one mile a second, though I'd have to calculate it out to be certain."

"One mile a second is still plenty," she said, impressed. "How is the energy stored?"

"Quantum degeneracy. The molecules of the accumulator are squeezed into low states. The pressure is maintained by a regenerative sub-field within the accumulator, which is, however, responsive to momentum transfer through the main barrier shell."

"You've just revised the entire concept of energy storage, you know," she said absently, "killed a dozen major industries and brought twenty new ones into existence. But as for the field, or screen, or shield, or whatever name you prefer——what is it? A region of warped space?"

"You can call it that if you want to, though strictly speaking, 'warped space' is a tautology at best, a meaningless noise at worst. I could show you the math——" Koskinen stopped short. He oughtn't. Not to this gang of criminals!

She relieved him by sighing; "I'd never understand. What little I ever knew about tensors has rusted away long ago. Let's keep this practical. I noticed today that you have a thermostatic unit built into the apparatus. You'd need it, obviously, since air can't get in or out of the screen. And you have some kind of oxygen recycler like nothing I ever saw."

"That's mostly derived from Martian technology," he admitted. "Exhaled carbon dioxide and water vapor circulate over a catalytic metal sponge surface which bleeds a little energy from the accumulator for a chemical process. Except for the small equilibrium concentration that your body needs, they're formed into solid carbohydrate and free oxygen. Trace exhalations like acetone—stinks—get converted to radicals attached to the carbohydrate.

"On Mars we included a unit that took care of organic wastes as well and reclaimed all excreted water. So then you only needed to take food along, and you could stay out on a field trip for weeks. But it was a heavy thing, that unit, and the principle was elementary, so we left it behind."

"I see," Vivienne nodded. "How could you

work, though, immobilized inside a barrier field?''

''We traveled on flatbed wagons or Martian sandsleds, drawn in a train by the electric tractors we'd taken along. Remote control robots did most of the actual specimen gathering. Toward the end, though, our engineers built a few of what we called walkies. One-man platforms with legs and hands, controlled by the rider, who could then go just about anywhere. In case of trouble, the shield could be expanded to enclose the machine as well as the man.

''Of course,'' Koskinen added thoughtfully, ''it was a makeshift. There's no reason why a shield can't be designed that'd fit a man like a thermsuit, only better, so he could walk and manipulate directly. It'd be a question of using a good many small generators, each responsive to the wearer's posture and motion. The total field at any instant would be the vector sum of the separate fields. However, that'll take a lot of engineering to do.''

''That's not the only possibility,'' she said with rising excitement. ''Spaceships, aircraft, even ground cars that haven't any hulls; just a potential shell generated when you need it. Vary the shape —turn your spaceship into your dome house— start really exploiting the minerals in the asteroid belt! A new kind of motor: push your ship forward by changing its energy potential. Why, you might be able to travel near the speed of light— if a faster-than-light drive isn't lurking somewhere in your spacewarp equations. A new way to get atomic energy, I'll bet; if you can hold the molecule in a degenerate state, you should be able to do the same for the nucleus. Perhaps you'll be able to convert any kind of matter into energy. No more fuel costs, no limit to the available power! Oh, Pete, your shield is only the beginning!''

He remembered where he was, jarringly, and said with returning grimness: ''It may be the end, with so many factions snatching after this thing.''

The light died in her. She leaned back. ''Yes,'' she said in a flat voice. ''That's very possible. Virtual invulnerability . . . yes, people have ripped each other apart for lesser prizes, haven't they?''

The servitor brought in a roast turkey with trimmings. Vivienne shook herself, as if she were cold. She flashed Koskinen a quick white smile. ''I'm sorry, Pete,'' she said. ''I didn't mean to talk shop so soon. Let's forget it for a while. I'd like to get acquainted with you as a person.'' Her voice dropped. ''Your kind of guy isn't any too common these days. Not anywhere in the world.''

They talked till far into the night.

VII

THE guard who escorted him waved Koskinen through the double door. The echoing concrete bleakness of the laboratory brought his isolation sharply back. Zigger and Vivienne were already there. The boss was asking her:

"You sure he didn't say nothing to you? Ever? Like maybe he was running a little show of his own in low-level somewhere, that he could of ducked out to take care of?"

Her mouth curled. "Don't be more moronic than you have to, Zigger. How could a hophead like Bones run anything except errands?"

"He's not a hophead."

"He's addicted to brain stimulation, isn't he?"

"That's not dope."

"I say it is."

Zigger lifted a hand as if to cuff her. She faced him rigidly. "How do you expect to locate Bones —that way?" she asked. He let the hand fall, turned about with a growl, and saw the new-comers.

"Argh! There you are!" The browless eyes glittered close to Koskinen. "C'mere. Grab him, Buck." One of the three guards present seized Koskinen's arms from behind. The grip was painful. Koskinen might have managed to break loose and get revenge, but the other two, and their master, had guns.

Zigger took a pair of channel pliers off the workbench. "I want you to understand something, Pete," he said, almost conversationally. "You've been caught. Nobody outside the Crater has any notion where you are. You're property. My property. I can do anything I feel like with you, and there won't be one damn thing you can do about it." The pliers closed on Koskinen's nose. "I can haul your beezer out by the roots, right now, this minute, if I want to." The jaws tightened until tears were stung from Koskinen's eyes. Zigger grinned voluptuously. "You got worse places than that to get squeezed," he said. "Or if I don't want to do any harm, I'll hook you into a nerve machine. That hurts maybe more. I've watched guys in it. When we're finished with you, we'll run you through the grinder. I keep cats, and you know what fresh meat costs."

As if with an effort, he tossed the pliers back. He had begun to sweat a little, and his voice wasn't as light as intended. "That's what I can do to property. Now, Vee, fix him up the way I told you."

Vivienne's face had gone altogether blank. She took a thick steel disc some three inches in diameter, suspended from a light chain, and hung it around Koskinen's neck. Picking a spotweld gun off the bench, she closed the links. He felt the heat on his skin, even through the asbestos paper she used to protect him. When she was done, he wore a locket he could not remove without cutting tools.

Zigger had explained while Vivienne worked: "This is to make sure you behave. You're gonna be helping our lady scientist with that force screen of yours. Showing her how it works, making more like it, maybe improving it some. So maybe you got ideas about getting the gadget on your back and switching the screen on, someplace where a laser can't get at you. Well, forget that. This here is a fulgurite capsule with a radio detonator. If I hear you're acting funny, I'll go press a button and blow your head off."

"Look out for stray signals, then," Koskinen snapped.

"Don't worry," Vivienne said. "The detonator is coded." She finished her job and released the chain, leaving the asbestos in place while the weld cooled.

"Let him go, Buck," Zigger said. Koskinen stumbled as his arms were released, rubbed his sore nose and scowled at them all.

Zigger beamed. "No hard feelings, Pete," he said. "I had to show you the bad side first. Now I can show you the good side. Care for a smoke? A happy pill? Got 'em right in my pocket here."

"No," Koskinen said.

"As long as you're a prisoner, you're property." Zigger said. "But the boys here aren't no property. They stick around because they know a good deal when they see one. I'd like to have

61

you join us, Pete. From your own free choice, I mean.

"Now don't look so horrified. I'm not a crook. You got to realize that. I'm a government myself. Sure. I make rules, and collect taxes, and take care of my people. What else is a government, huh? What'd Washington ever do for you that I can't do better? You want money, good food, good housing, fun and games? You can have 'em, right here, starting today, if you want. You wouldn't live in the Crater your whole life, neither. Change your face and you can go anywhere. I keep some mighty nice apartments, hunting lodges, villas, yachts, whatchamacallit, here and there around the world. I'll have a lot more once we've got those shields of yours ready. A whale of a lot more. Use your imagination, boy, and see what we might get us in the next few years. Want in on the game?"

Koskinen remained silent.

Zigger slapped his back. "Think it over, Pete," he said jovially. "Meanwhile, work hard and be good. So long." He went out. The guards followed him. The door closed behind them.

Vivienne struck a cigarette, sat down on a stool and smoked in short ferocious puffs. Koskinen wandered about the room. The bomb was a lump at the base of his throat. He glanced at the monitor screen. Someone was watching him, of course, from elsewhere in this warren. He felt like making an impolite gesture at the watchman, but decided not to. The shield unit lay on the bench. He fiddled nervously with the controls.

62

After a while, Vivienne stirred. "Well," she said.

He didn't answer.

"I'm sorry about that thing," she said. "I got my orders. I can get away with a lot, but a direct order from the boss——"

"Sure," he said.

"As for the rest . . . what he did . . . I suppose Zigger's no worse than the average gang baron. Probably not even much worse than any other government. He's right about being a government, you know."

"They don't practice torture in Washington," he muttered.

"I'm not so sure," she said bitterly.

He glanced at her, surprised. She hadn't said much about her past, for all the talking they had done. He gathered that she came from a well-to-do family and had gotten an education commensurate with her intelligence at a private school; that was interrupted by the war, and she had had a few bad years afterward, first in the refugee hordes and then as a semi-slave in a guerrilla band, until the police wiped them out and turned her over to the Institute. It gave her room, board, medical treatment, psychiatric help, and training in science. "I should think you'd be the last person to preach anarchism," he said.

"Or archism, for that matter." Her smile was stiff. "I've been on the receiving end of both conditions." With a slight shake, as if to drive off her thoughts: "About Zigger. He was in a tough mood. Worried about Bones disappearing."

"Who?"

"Neff's pal. Remember, there were two guys in that restaurant? Neff went out to the fake taxi and captured you. Bones tailed you to the door."

"Oh, yes. The runt. I remember."

"He went back into town yesterday. He was supposed to report in by nightfall—Zigger had a job for him—but he hasn't shown yet and they can't find any trace of him out there."

"Violence?"

"Maybe. Though Zigger's people are more apt to dish that out than take it. Bones might have run afoul of a boy pack, of course, or even a raiding party from New Haven Crater. We've been fighting a sort of war with them for control of Yonkers low-level—— Oh, the devil with this." Vivienne ground out her cigarette. "Everything's so sickening. Why doesn't the official government get off the dollar and clean out these pest holes?"

"I suppose they will in time," Koskinen said. "There've been too many other things to handle first, though. Maintaining the Protectorate takes so much money and energy that——"

"Don't talk to me about the Protectorate!" she burst out.

He gaped at her. She broke into a shiver. Her eyes, close to tears, looked past him and past the wall. The nails bit into her palms.

"Why, what's wrong?" he ventured, and took a step toward her.

"If I believed in God," she said through her teeth, "I'd think he hated us—our country, our whole tribe—and saddled us with the Norris Doctrine so we'd maintain our own damnation and save him the trouble!''

''Huh? But . . . I mean, Vee, what else would you do? Do you want to fight a third thermonuclear war?''

Echoing in the back of his head were the words they had made him memorize in his current affairs class at the Institute:

''——*the future security of the United States. Therefore, from this moment henceforth, no other national state shall be permitted to keep arms or armed forces beyond what is needed for internal policing. Any attempt to manufacture, assemble, recruit, or otherwise prepare forces suitable for aggressive action, shall be an act of war against the United States, and the individuals responsible shall be arrested and tried as war criminals by an American military court. In order to prevent the secret accumulation of such forces, the United States will exercise an unlimited right of inspection. Otherwise national sovereignty will be fully respected and the United States guarantees the integrity of all national frontiers as of the date of this Proclamation. The United States recognizes that nations may adjust such frontiers by mutual agreement, and that the people of any nation may change their form of government by lawful or even revolutionary means. However, the United States reserves to itself the right of judgment as to whether any given change is consonant with its own security, and shall not permit changes which it deems potentially dangerous to its own and the world's future.*''

Congress, the Supreme Court, and subsequent Presidents had elaborated the Norris Doctrine until the theory was a lawyer's paradise, Koskinen reminded himself. But the practice was simple enough for anyone to understand. The Americans maintained the last military services on Earth, and brought them to bear whenever the President decided the national interest required action. The day-to-day details of inspection, intelligence operations, evaluation of data, and advice to the executive, were in the hands of the Bureau of Military Security.

Vivienne didn't answer Koskinen's question.

"We're not perfect," he said, "and, well, it's no fun being a cop . . . and it's made us unpopular . . . but who else could be trusted with the job?"

She looked at him, then, and said: "MS tried to kill you."

"Well . . . okay, they did." Argument stiffened his opinions. "They wouldn't have if . . . I mean, I'd rather have been cleanly shot than gone to some Chinese torture chamber . . . or come here, you know!"

"They killed my husband," she said.

He fell silent.

"Want to hear the story?" she asked without tone, turning her gaze from him again. "After my graduation I got a foreign service job, assistant science attaché, and drew an assignment to Brazil. Janio was an engineer there. Sweet and a little bit crazy and very young—oh, how young! Not much less than me in years, actually. But Brazil didn't get hit very hard in the war, and he'd

66

scarcely seen anything of the aftermath. He hadn't been poisoned, as I'd been, and with him I finally began to feel clean again. We used to go bird-watching on the river. . . .

"There was this hothead conspiracy. MS had vetoed a plan to mine some uranium deposits in the Serra Dourado, on the grounds that they didn't have inspectors enough to make sure that some of the stuff wasn't smuggled out and turned into bombs——"

Her voice trailed off. "Well, they don't," Koskinen said. Helpless before her emotion, he thought vaguely of turning the conversation into safer channels. "Inspection is a highly technical job. There aren't many qualified men available. And even one country is such a big place. How do you think the Chinese, for instance, keep that net-work of agents and agitators going? The Chinese government disowns the organization officially, and the whole world knows they support it clan-destinely, and there's nothing we can do because we haven't got people enough to govern China ourselves."

"Uh-huh," she said dully. "In China there's at least a fairly honest and fairly competent govern-ment, however much they hate us behind those bland smiles. Most other places, we just prop up a bunch of corrupt do-nothings, because we know they won't make trouble . . . and never mind whether their people have a life worth the effort of living. Oh, yes, we talk non-interference in foreign internal affairs; but in practice—I've been in the diplomatic service, I tell you. I know."

He sighed. "I'm sorry. Didn't mean to interrupt."

"Thanks for that apology, Pete. You remind me of Janio, a little. . . . Oh. What happened. Those mines would have given work to a lot of hungry paupers. Some nuts decided to overthrow the Brazilian government, establish a new one that wasn't a puppet, and talk back to the Yankees. The conspiracy flopped. An amateur job. MS and the Brazilian secret service caught everybody. Including Janio, who was not one of them. I should know that too, shouldn't I? My own Johnny! I knew where he spent his time. But he had been angry about the Serra Dourado business, along with a lot of other things. He was a proud guy, and he wanted his country to go her own way. He'd spoken his piece—what does our First Amendment say?—and it's true that some of his friends were in the plot.

"They brought us to Washington for trial. I wasn't arrested myself, but I came along, of course. There were interrogations under drugs. I thought that would clear Johnny. Instead, someone I'd never met before swore in court that he'd seen my husband at some of those meetings. I called him a liar under oath. I *knew* Johnny'd been with me on several of those exact dates. You know the funny little associations that fix something in your memory. We must have been camped on that Amazon island the weekend of the 23rd because we saw twenty-three macaws fly by, emerald green in a pink sunrise, and he said the gods were providing me with a calendar because they also thought I was beautiful. . . . That sort of thing.

"So they found him guilty. And shot him. And I was charged with perjury. But they gave me probation. Scientists are valuable and so forth. One evening, a year or so later, I met a business executive with high government connections at a party in Manhattan. He got so drunk that he spilled to me why Johnny had been orbited. The PI exam had shown he was 'a strongly potential insurrectionist.' That is, he might someday get fed up with being shoved around in his own country, and do something about it. Better kill him now. 'Before he helps build a bomb, or finds one of the big missiles still hidden here and there with all records on them lost. He could kill millions of us,' the executive said. My Johnny!

"The next day I went down to low-level. Mostly I wanted to get away, lost, killed if I was lucky. But I got picked up by Zigger instead. Kidnap, I suppose, technically; but it didn't seem to matter much; at any rate, it's one way of striking back at them."

Her words faded. She sat quiet, the tall body slumped, until finally she took forth a cigarette and struck it. But after a few puffs she let it burn out between her fingers.

"I'm dreadfully sorry," Koskinen whispered.

"Thanks," she said roughly. "My turn to apologize, though. I didn't mean to unload my troubles on you."

"I suppose any body of men gets . . . excessive . . . when it has power."

"Yes, no doubt. When the power isn't restricted, at least."

"And MS can't very well be restricted, if it's to do its work. Although the shield effect might make MS unnecessary. You could shield against atomic bombs, given a large enough unit."

She stirred and looked at him with a hint of life. "Hardly practical," she said. Her voice was unsteady, now and then she bit her lip, but she found impersonal phrases. "Especially since a bomb could be smuggled in piecemeal, assembled inside the target area. Or there are other nasty weapons, bacteria, gas. Don't get me wrong, Pete. I hate Marcus and his MS goons as much as anyone has ever hated. But I'm not so naive I think any other country would maintain the peace better. And one way or another, I suppose the job does have to be done; because any sovereign state is a monster, without morals or brains, that'd incinerate half the human race to get its sovereign way."

"An international organization——"

"Too late now," she sighed. "Who could we trust?" With a stubborn striving to be fair: "Besides, we do have a society of our own here, a way we prefer to live, the same as Brazil or China has. We won't surrender that to some world policeman; we can't, and remain what we are. And yet I don't see how a world police force could be made workable without a world community. So maybe the Pax Americana is the only answer."

He stared down at the unit on the bench, remembering how Elkor had blessed it on the day the ship departed. The Martian had endured all the agonies of delayed hibernation so he could bid his humans farewell. "This thing, though," Koskinen protested. "There must be some way to use it. The majority of people who died in either atomic war were actually not killed by blast or the immediate radiation. Firestorms and fall-out were what got them; later on, anarchy or disease. A shield unit would protect you against those things, as well as gas and——"

"Sure," Vivienne said. "That's why Zigger wants to outfit his bully boys with your screens. There'd be no stopping him then. In ten years he'd own low-level from here to California, and a good part of the legitimate world too."

"And we're supposed to make them for him?" Koskinen cried.

"And improve them, in time. If we don't, he can hire engineers to do so. The job doesn't look extremely difficult."

"No. . . . I can't. I've got to get this to the police!"

"Which means to MS," she said slowly.

"Well—I suppose so."

"Which means Director Hugh Marcus. What do you imagine he'll do then—remembering Janio?"

Koskinen stood quietly. She pursued pitilessly, and he did not think it was because she, like him, had suddenly remembered the monitor: "If not Marcus, then somebody else. You simply haven't thought out the implications. Invulnerability! Give anyone who has power, from Zigger on up through Marcus or the dictator of China . . . give anyone who has power over other human beings invulnerability, and you free that power from the last trace of accountability. From then on, anything goes.

"I'd rather Zigger got this thing," she finished. Her mouth was drawn taut. She fumbled out another cigarette and made a stabbing gesture with it. "All he wants, really, is plunder. Not the souls of the whole human race."

VIII

KOSKINEN awoke. What was that?

Maybe nothing. A dream, from which he'd escaped before it got too ghastly. He had perforce taken a pill to sleep, but that must have worn off by now. The luminous clock said 0415 EDST. Otherwise he lay in total blackness. And soundlessness, apart from the murmur in the ventilation grille. These thick walls effectively insulated every apartment. If an outside noise had roused him, it must have been loud indeed.

He rolled over and tried to doze off again, but instead he grew completely wakeful. What Vivienne had said today, and her tone and expression and whole posture, had disturbed him more than he wanted to admit.

I wouldn't know the score. Not really. My youth was spent in what amounted to a fancy boarding school. I never encountered outside, day-to-day reality. Not that the professors lied to us, or any such thing. They told us conditions were hard, and that we'd have to buck poverty, ignorance, tyranny, greed, and hate. But I see now their understanding of the situation was childish. They accepted their political opinions readymade, from official sources, because their work kept them too busy to do anything else.

I might have gone into the world with the rest of my classmates and had my nose rubbed in a few facts. But instead I shipped out to Mars. Now I come home, and the truth confronts me. And not gradually, so I can get used to it and accept it as sad but unavoidable. In one big brutal dose. I want to vomit it up again.

Only what is the truth? he thought wearily. *Who's right? What's the way out? If any.*

He had spent the day in an emotionally stunned fashion, finding some anodyne in drawing up, with Vivienne's help, the diagrams and specifications for the shield unit. There seemed no choice but to obey Zigger. Though they hadn't yet completed the job, several more hours would suffice. Lying now in bed, his fists clenched, he thought: *I've been pushed around too bloody often. Time I started some pushing of my own.* But the explosive locket and chain were like a hand around his neck. Maybe sometime, somewhere along the line, he could secretly make a cage to screen out the signal that would touch off the fulgurite. Maybe. Not soon, though. He'd have to bide his time, and watch his chance, and eat dirt——

A dull boom resounded. The floor quivered.

Koskinen sprang out of bed. His heart skipped a beat and began galloping. Hoy—wasn't that a siren? He found the light switch. In that sudden illumination the room looked altogether bare. He tried the door. Locked, of course. He laid his ear against the panel and could just hear shouts, running feet . . . yes, certainly a siren, wailing elsewhere in the caverns.

He switched on the phone. It didn't respond. Were nonessential circuits cut off for the emergency, or had the central been destroyed? Another crash trembled through rock.

Raid! But who?

Zigger. Koskinen broke into a chill sweat. If a desperate Zigger pressed one certain button. . . . He discovered he was trying to snap the chain with his hands. Swiftly, futilely, he searched the apartment for anything that might cut metal. Nothing. He put on some clothes, set his teeth, and paced the floor, waiting.

The racket increased outside. Another explosion came, and another. But he heard no more people go by. The fight must be some ways off, then. He couldn't do a thing except await events. He tried to recall his parents, and Elkor, and daydreams he had once nourished, but he was too tense. *Stupid,* he scolded himself. *If that bomb goes off, you'll never know it.* The realization did little to calm him.

A louder crash yet. The lights flickered and dimmed. The ventilator fan whirred to a halt.

Koskinen's mouth felt like Martian dust. He started to the cubby for a drink of water. The door opened. He whirled and crouched back.

Vivienne Cordeiro stepped through, closing the door behind her. She wore a coverall. There was a pistol in her hand and an ungainly bundle on her back with a cloth draped over it. Her eyes were narrowed, the broad nostrils flared and her mouth bore a tight grin.

"There!" she panted. "Take this." She slipped the thing off her shoulders. The cloth fell away and Koskinen looked upon the shield unit. "A little heavy for me to run with."

"What——what——" he staggered toward her.

"Get it on, you clotbrain! We'll be lucky to escape as is."

Strength resurged. He heaved the metal up and put his arms through the straps. "What's happened?"

"Raiding party. Big one, with military equipment. Chinese, according to one guy at a monitor. They lobbed in a couple of small HE missiles from the air, which shook up our ack-ack long enough for them to land. Now they're blowing their way in past our defenses. We're equipped to stand off another gang or even a police siege, but not stuff like they've got!" She tucked the cloth firmly about his burden. "Into the cubby, now."

"What?"

She dragged him by the hand. "Everybody knows what you look like. But without those whiskers, you've got a fair chance of not being noticed. Quick!" She handed him the depple.

He ran it over his face, recognizing his chin again with a faint shock. Not having a very strong growth of beard, he could expect to be smooth-cheeked for a week or so without further plucking. The desensitizer spray felt cool on his skin.

Vivienne kept on talking: "I can guess how they did it, the Chinese. They knew approximately where you landed, so they sent a good many

agents in to try and pick up your trail. Must have
identified Bones in town—everybody in the neigh-
borhood knows who the Crater people are—and
put the snatch on him." She spared a sigh for poor
old Bones and the treatment which was doubtless
used to make him guide the attack. "Obviously
they're shooting their wad. Every military weapon
they've stockpiled in this country, secretly, over
the years, must be out there. It's worth it, though.
A China equipped with barrier screens could tell
MS where to get off, build a nuclear arsenal again,
and probably blackmail us out of Asia."

Koskinen shuddered.

"I can't take the chance they'll succeed," Vivienne said. "Especially since it looks as if they will
get in here. I don't want another war either. So I
got my gun and let myself into the lab. What plans
we drew today are ashes now."

"Wait." Koskinen remembered. He touched his
throat.

She laughed, a short humorless bark. "Yes, I
thought of that too. There's a direct passage between Zigger's suite and mine. He thought he had
the only key, but I made myself a duplicate long
ago. And I know where he keeps stuff like this.
The minute he went out to command the defense,
I popped in." Briefly she drew a small flat case
with a button and a safety catch from another
pocket. "Here's the detonator."

Koskinen snatched for it. She sidestepped him.
"No, you don't. Now let's go. There isn't much
time."

She opened the door first and peered into the
hall. "Okay. Everything's clear." They stepped

77

through. A guard sprawled outside. He had been shot in the head. Vivienne nodded. "Yes," she said. "Wasn't any other way to get in. Gimme a hand." They dragged him into the room and locked the door again with his key.

"Burned your bridges, eh?" Koskinen asked. In this corridor full of explosions, machine gun snarl, smoke and shock, he felt oddly callous about the murder.

"No," said the woman. "My bridges were burned for me quite some time ago. The day they killed Johnny. C'mon, this way."

They crossed a glideway which had gone motionless. The air already seemed stagnant and cooling. The sounds of battle grew fainter. Koskinen's pulse leaped when a squad of guards came loping past, but they paid him no special heed. Vivienne led him on down a side hall with plain, unnumbered doors. "Mostly they're storerooms," she said, "but this here. . . . Take the lead. Keep your hand on the switch and be ready to shield yourself when I tell you."

Beyond the room, another door gave onto a steep upward ramp. Koskinen's footfalls pattered between bare walls. His breathing was loud in his ears. He felt the strain in thigh and shoulder muscles, caught the sour smell of his own sweat. The lights were few and dim against whitewashed flatnesses.

Rounding a continuous curve, he came to the end without warning. An armored door blocked the passage ahead, where a machine gun pit held two sentries. Their helmets and gas masks made them unhuman. "Hold it, you two!" one called. The gun swiveled toward Koskinen.

"Shield," Vivienne hissed. He threw the switch. Silence clamped upon him. Vivienne, at his back, drew her gun and fired, full automatic. The first soldier lurched and fell. The machine gun raved, noiselessly for Koskinen. Bullets dropped at his feet. Vivienne continued to fire from behind him. The gunner collapsed.

She ran to the pit, looked at the men, and waved to her companion. He snapped off his shield and joined her. The blood glistened impossibly bright. This killing sickened him, perhaps because he had seen it done. "Did you have to?" he strangled.

Her nod was curt. "They'd never have let us by without a pass. Don't waste any grief on these bums. They did plenty of assassinations in their day." She pulled a control switch. "We've got to hurry. They probably sent an alarm."

A motor whirred. The door swung ponderously open. Blackness gaped beyond. Vivienne took a flashlight from one guard's belt and scrambled over unfinished rock—a short, curved tunnel that roared and echoed with battle noise. Its entrance was camouflaged by a giant boulder. Koskinen halted in the stone's shadow and looked out.

Three big, lean aircraft hovered against the red sky. He could discern several others on the black surface near the main entrance; they were little more than metallic gleams, seen by lightning-like bursts as ground combat spilled across the crater bowl. Smoke hazed the scene as much as the night did. Koskinen was chiefly aware of confusion. But he distinguished the sounds: bang, crack, staccato rattle, then a rumbling as high explosive went off down in the tunnels.

"The Chinese must be gambling the police will figure this for only another gang clash," Vivienne said. "If the cops do try to intervene, naturally they'll be shot down. They haven't got any stuff to compare with that there. So then MS and the Army will be called in . . . but that'll take a little while. The Chinese must hope to be away with their booty—you, for one item—before matters progress that far."

"Where can we go?" he asked, stupefied at what he saw.

"Away. Come." She led him over a nearly invisible track that wound toward the rim. He stumbled after her. Now and then he fell, taking cuts and bruises which stung abominably. But the discovery and capture which terrified him didn't happen. They mounted the crater lip, scrambled down through snags and skeletons of blasted structures, and so into the labyrinth called lowlevel.

IX

THEY stopped in an alley. Blank brick walls enclosed two sides and filled it with gloom. Light trickled from gray rectangles at either end, where the streets could be seen, empty at this hour save when the wind blew a dust cloud along or a rattling scrap of paper. Overhead ran a pneumotube and a tangle of power lines; beyond, the sky-glow. They had come too far to hear the battle at the Crater, if it was still going on. Midnight growling and pounding, automatic machines, automatic traffic, made a background which smothered any remote noises that might otherwise have been heard. The air was cold and smelled faintly of sulfur compounds.

Koskinen sat down opposite Vivienne and let exhaustion overwhelm him. After a long time he was able to look across at her, where she huddled in the murk as another shadow, and say, "What next?"

"I don't know," she answered in a dead voice.

"The police——"

"No!" The violence of her denial shocked them both toward greater wakefulness. "Let me think a while," she said. She struck a cigarette on the wall—he heard the tiny *scrit* through all the city's grumble—and drew smoke till the red end flared into brilliance.

"Who else have we got to turn to?" he argued. "Another gang boss? No, thanks."

"Indeed not," she said. "Especially since the hue and cry will really be out, once MS picks up the pieces at the Crater and gets some idea of what happened. The word will get around. No baron will dare do anything but turn us in if he finds us."

"So let's go to MS ourselves."

"How many times do you have to get kicked in the teeth before you learn not to walk behind that particular horse?" she snapped.

"What do you mean? Okay, I admit they've killed. But——"

"Do you want to spend your life incommunicado?"

"Huh?"

"Oh, they may simply wipe your memory. Which runs a grave risk of disintegrating the entire personality. Mnemotechnics isn't the exact science it pretends to be." He thought she quailed in the darkness. "Me, I'd rather be put in a dungeon for life than have their probes go into my brain. A prisoner can always find some way to kill herself decently."

"But why? *I'm* not the rebel type."

"Figure it out. At present you, and only you on Earth, know how the screen generator works. A

man like Marcus, who'd cold-bloodedly frame
and shoot an innocent person because he might
someday make trouble . . . a man like that won't
want to risk the secret getting out of his control. I
don't say Marcus would actually plan on making
himself the military dictator of the United
States—not right away—but that's where he'd
end, step by step. Because how do you effectively
oppose a man who's got strong convictions, and
power, and invulnerability?''

"You're exaggerating," he said.

"Shut up," she said. "Let me think."

The wind whimpered. A train screamed down
some track not far away. Vivienne's cigarette end
waxed and waned.

"I know one spot we might aim for," she said
at length. "Zigger has—had—a place upstate, under a different name. It's stocked with supplies
and weapons, like all his places. Got a special
phone system, too—a shielded underground cable
that sneaks into a public circuit several miles off,
so you can buzz your friends without danger of
having your call tapped or traced. We can lie low
there for a while, and maybe get in touch with
some reliable—Brazilian?—anyway, try to get
ourselves smuggled out of the country."

"And then what?" he challenged.

"I don't know. Maybe throw your unit and
plans into the sea and hide out in some backwoods
area for the rest of our lives. Or maybe we can
think of something better. Don't bug me, Pete.
I'm about ready to cave in as is."

"No," Koskinen said.

"What?" She stirred.

"Sorry. Perhaps I am too trusting. Or perhaps you aren't trusting enough. But when I signed for the Mars trip, I took an oath to support the Constitution." He climbed achingly to his feet. "I'm going to call MS to come get me."

She rose too. "No, you don't!"

He clapped a hand on his generator switch. "Don't draw that gun," he said. "I can shield myself faster than you can shoot, and outwait you."

She stepped back, reached in a pocket and pulled forth the detonator. "Can you outwait this?" she countered unsteadily.

He gasped and made a move toward her. "Stop where you are!" she shrilled. He thought he heard a snick as she thumbed off the safety. "I'll kill you before I let you turn that thing over to him!"

Koskinen stood very still. "Would you?" he breathed.

"Yes . . . it's that important . . . it really is, Pete. You talked about your oath. D-d-don't you see—Marcus—he'd destroy what's left of . . . of the Constitution?" She began to cry, he heard her, but he could make out in the night that she still clutched the detonator.

"You've got everything wrong," he pleaded. "How do you know Marcus would act that way —or be able to if he wanted? He doesn't even have Cabinet rank. There're other branches of government, Congress, the courts, the President. . . . I can't outlaw myself just because—an opinion— you aren't giving them a chance, Vee!"

Silence fell between them again. He waited, thinking of many things, feeling his aloneness.

Until she caught her breath with a gulp and said in a thin little voice:

"Maybe. I can't tell for sure. It's your machine, and your life, and—I suppose I could always go hide. But I wish you'd really satisfy yourself . . . before you walk into their parlor . . . I wish you would. Once you're there it'd be too late. And you're too good for what might happen to you."

Dave, he remembered. For a long while he stood, shoulders hunched beneath his burden, thinking about Dave Abrams. *Anyway, I've been too passive. That's a shirking of responsibility, I suppose—but mainly, I'm fed up to the eyeballs with being pushed around.*

A minor part of him was surprised to note how resolution brought back physical strength. He spoke quite steadily. "Okay, Vee, I'll do what you say. I think I know how, too."

She slipped the detonator back into her pocket and followed him mutely to the street. They walked several blocks before turning a corner and seeing a cluster of darkened shops with a public call booth outside. She gave him some coins—he had none in this suit—and posted herself by the door. Her cheeks gleamed wet in the dull lamplight, but her lips had grown firm again.

Koskinen called first for a taxi. Then he punched for local MS headquarters. The telltale glowed crimson; government agencies always recorded calls. He didn't make a visual transmission. No sense in betraying his changed appearance before he must.

"Bureau of Military Security," said a woman's voice.

Koskinen stiffened. "Listen," he said. "This is urgent. Get your tape immediately to whoever's in charge. This is Peter Koskinen speaking, from the USAAS *Franz Boas*. I know you're looking for me, and I'm back at large with the thing you're after. But I'm not certain I can trust you. I tried to call a shipmate of mine, David Abrams, a couple of nights ago, and learned you'd hauled him in. That sounds suspicious to me. Maybe I'm wrong about that. But what I've got is too important to hand over blindly.

"I'm leaving now. I'll call again in half an hour from somewhere else. At that time I want you to have a hookup ready which will include Abrams. Understand? I want to see Abrams personally and satisfy myself that he's okay and not being unjustifiably held. Got me?"

He switched off and stepped from the booth. The taxi was already there, as he had hoped. Vivienne had prudently tucked her gun and holster into the coverall; the driver wouldn't have come near if he saw that. As it was, he wore a helmet and had a needler just like Neff's friend—dear God, only two nights ago? Standard equipment for low-level hackies, evidently. Koskinen and Vivienne got in. The driver said into a microphone—a blankout panel, doubtless bulletproof, hid him from the rear seat—"Where to?"

Koskinen was caught off guard. Vivienne said quickly: "Brooklyn, and fast."

"Got to swing wide of the Crater, ma'am. Wider than usual, I mean. Some kinda ruckus going on there, so Control's re-routed traffic."

"That's okay." Koskinen leaned back as much as the unit he wore permitted. They swung aloft. MS would probably have a car at the booth within minutes, but that would be too late. They might then check with Control, but the chances were that the computer would already have removed the fact that this one cab had stopped at that one corner from its circulating memory. Investigation of the various taxi companies would take more time than was available. *So I am on top of the situation*, Koskinen thought. *Barely*.

"Brooklyn," the driver said after a short while. "Where now?"

"Flatbush tube station," Vivienne instructed.

"Hey, I'll getcha anywhere in the borough as cheap's the tubeway, now we're here, and a lot quicker."

"You heard the lady," Koskinen said. The driver muttered something uncomplimentary but obeyed. Vivienne gave him a handsome tip when they left. "Otherwise he might get so mad he'd check with the cops, hoping we are wanted," she explained as she boarded the escalator with her companion.

The gate took money and admitted them. They entered the tube, stepped onto the belt and found a seat. There were a few other passengers—workmen, a priest, several Orientals who looked out of withdrawn eyes at the Western gut down which they traveled—but not many. The city wouldn't really awaken for another hour.

Vivienne regarded Koskinen a while. "You're looking better now," she remarked.

"I feel a little better, somehow," he admitted. He slipped off the screen unit and laid it at his feet.

"Wish I could say the same." Her own eyes were bloodshot and edged with blackness. "I'm tired, though." She sighed. "Tired down into my bones. Not just the chase tonight. All the years behind me. Was there ever a small girl named Veevee in a room with blue ducks on the wallpaper? It feels more like something I read once in an old book."

He took her hand, wordlessly, and dared slip the other arm across her shoulder. The dark head leaned against him. "I'm sorry, Pete," she said. "I don't want to go soupy on you. But do you mind if I cry a little? I'll be very quiet."

He held her closer. No one else paid any particular attention. He remembered the oneness of the ship's crew, and of the Martians, and eventually with the Martians—not a loss of freedom, rather an unspoken belongingness which gave meaning to a freedom that would otherwise have been empty . . . perhaps the grisliest thing he had found on Earth so far was the isolation of human beings from each other.

But what else could result, when a man was one atom in a deaf, dumb, blind, automated machine?

They rode with no special destination until his watch said it was about time to call MS again. Occasionally Koskinen switched the seat onto cross-tube belts chosen at random. Vivienne had dozed a few minutes and seemed refreshed thereby. She walked springily with him to the gate when they got off.

Below the escalator, he looked around. They had come into a better district. The buildings on their side of the street were fairly new, with curving setback walls of tinted plastic, broad windows, and balconies. Across the avenue marched the cyclone fence that enclosed the parkscape around a Center. That pile dominated the scene like a mountain, but Koskinen hardly noticed. He was too struck by the grounds themselves, grass ablaze with green, flowerbeds of red and blue and yellow, the graciousness of trees, beneath a sky that had turned pale in the east. *I'd almost forgotten that Earth is still the most beautiful planet*, he thought.

A uniformed guard watched them idly from behind the fence. A few early—or very late—ground cars whispered along the street; trucks and trains weren't allowed here. There was a cab stand close by, so no reason to phone for getaway transportation again.

Why getaway? Koskinen resisted. *Why not simply a ride down to the MS office?*

He wet his lips, made himself ignore his pulse, and entered the corner booth. Vivienne waited outside, guarding the shield generator. Her gaze never left him. He punched the number.

"Bureau of——"

"Koskinen," he said roughly. "Are you prepared to talk to me?"

"Oh! One moment." Click. A man's voice rapped: "This is Colonel Ausland. If you'll go on visual, Koskinen, I'll switch you over to Director Marcus himself."

"Okay." Koskinen put in the extra coin. "But

bear this in mind, I don't have the machine. If you trace this call and snatch me, my confederate has instructions to take off for parts unknown. Unknown to me too, I'd better add.''

The screen showed him an indignant face which quickly gave way to another—heavy, bushy-browed, with distinguished gray hair, Hugh Marcus in Washington. Koskinen had seen so many news pictures in his youth that he recognized the man at once.

"Hello, there," said Marcus quite gently. "What's the matter? What are you scared of, son?"

"You," Koskinen said.

"Well, you've obviously had some rough experiences, but——"

"Quiet! I know damn well I haven't much time before your agents can get to where I am. I've been treated pretty high-handedly, Marcus, and I want some assurance from a person I can trust that it was only because of circumstances and not because your bureau has grown too big for its britches. Got Dave Abrams ready to talk to me?"

"Wait a minute. Wait a minute." Marcus raised one large manicured hand. "Don't start off half-programmed like that. We took Abrams into custody, yes. For his own protection, same as we wanted to protect you. He's perfectly okay——"

"Let him tell me so. Quick, there!"

Marcus flushed but continued mildly: "Why Abrams in particular? It so happens we can't bring him on such short notice. We tucked him away in a Rocky Mountains hideout, and saw no reason why he and the agents guarding him shouldn't get in some fishing. So they're off in the woods, and atmospherics are such that their talkie sets evidently won't reach our nearest closed-circuit relay.''

"*I* say you've shot him full of mind dope and couldn't wring him dry that fast. So long, Marcus." Koskinen reached for the switch.

"Wait a second!" Marcus cried. "Will you talk to Carl Holmboe? We've got him standing by for you, safe and sound.''

The engineering officer—Koskinen swayed on knees gone rubbery. "Sure," he husked. "Put him on.''

The image changed. A balding walrus-mustached man regarded Koskinen, in his own screen, with a dazed expression.

"Hello, Carl," Koskinen said softly.

"Oh. Pete." Holmboe's eyes flickered sideways. Did a guard with a gun stand beyond pickup range? "What's got into you?''

"I'm not sure," Koskinen said. "How're they treating you?''

"Fine. Shouldn't they be? I'm fine.''

"You don't look it.''

"Pete——" Holmboe swallowed. "Come on home, Pete. I don't know what the score is, except that you insist on being told they won't hurt you at MS. Well, they won't.''

Koskinen paused. Stillness hummed from the phone. Through the booth windows, he saw the western stars go out as the sun came closer. Vivienne had not stirred from her place.

He forced tongue and larynx into those deep croaks which were the closest men would ever come to High Martian Vocal. *"Carl, Sharer-of Hopes, is there a reality in what you attest?"*

.Holmboe started. His face turned still whiter. "Don't call me that!"

"Why should I not name you Sharer-of-Hopes, as our whole band named each other that night in the shrine with the Martians and the Philosopher's Sending? I will come to you if you tell me in the pledge language that there is no wrongness intended."

Holmboe tried to speak and could not.

"Sharer-of-Hopes, I know the danger to yourself," Koskinen said. *"Were that the only aspect of this plenum, I would come at once. But I believe, in the night way I learned on Elkor's tower, that more is at hazard than life."*

"Go swiftly and far," Holmboe told him.

He shook himself, leaned forward, and barked in English: "Lay off that stuff, Pete. You must be having a brain typhoon or something, the way you're acting. If you want me to swear in Martian that it's safe to come here, okay, I've sworn. So quit making a jackass of yourself."

"S-sure. I'll come," Koskinen said. "I, uh, I have to stop and get the machine from the person I left it with. But then I'll go straight to the nearest MS office." He drew a breath. His throat felt thick, as if he had swallowed the bomb that was chained beneath it, and his eyes stung. "Thanks, Carl," he said somehow.

"Yeah. I'll be seeing you."

I hope so.

Koskinen blanked the screen. Maybe Carl was off the hook now. Maybe he'd gained a little time for himself to . . . to do whatever came next. Existence grant that this be. There had been so much death.

He left the booth. Vivienne seized his hand. "What's the word, Pete?"

He picked up the unit. "Let's get away while we can," he answered sharply.

X

SHE stood silent for a little while. The sun, not yet visible, touched the heights of the Center with rose and gold and filled the street with light. Traffic had not increased much; the residents of an area like this seldom needed to get up early. Here there was no gut-growl of megalopolis, like that which never ended in the slums. Rather, the city sounds were like a gentle great breathing. Against that background, Vivienne made him think of a dark angel prowling just beyond the walls of that paradise which had cast her out.

"Where?" she asked. "Upstate, Zigger's place?"

"God, I don't know. I hate to . . . do nothing but run away. We need help."

Her laugh was sarcastic. "Who's going to give it?" She caught his hand. "Come on, Pete! MS'll trace that call. They'll have somebody here inside of minutes."

"I told them I was going to them."

"They'll check here on principle. Come *on!*"

Light flared off a window in the immense building opposite. Koskinen blinked. It was as if the sun itself had flashed him a signal. "Yes!" he almost shouted.

"What?" Wide eyes, gold-flecked brown, searched his face. "You thought of something?"

"Uh-huh." He started walking rapidly toward the taxi stand.

The cabs were new and shiny here, the drivers unarmed. "That line doesn't enter the slums," Vivienne warned.

"We're not going to the slums."

"Hacks can be dangerous, Pete. They receive all public announcements. As soon as MS broadcasts an alarm for us, the cabbies will see it. Ours might very well remember us——"

"We haven't much choice, I'm afraid. The tubeways are too slow, if MS should decide to go directly after us. And they can be stopped, can't they? I don't want to sit trapped in a tunnel, waiting for a squad to investigate my coach."

Her mind sprang ahead of him. "We want to go somewhere top-level, right?" she asked. He nodded. "Okay," she said, "I'll take a chance that you know what you're doing, because there isn't time to argue. But let's act typical rather than unusual. We can pretty well conceal our faces, too. Then I don't think we will be remembered. Here, give me that generator." She took it easily in one hand. "I'd likelier carry a piece of apparatus than you. I'm a girl you picked up while slumming, you see, just after I'd gotten off work. Lord knows I look it, in this outfit. And you still look fairly respectable; that dark suit you're wearing doesn't show how dirty you really are.''

"What do you mean?'' he asked, bewildered.

The sky was now so bright that he could see her flush. But she said in an impersonal hurry, "We've been touring the low-level taverns to-night." At his continued gaping: "Look, you fool, you're the wastrel son of a multi-billionaire. There are enough of that breed around! Play the part . . . oh, hell, you poor bumbling innocent, follow my lead.''

They neared the taxis. Koskinen's mind boggled when Vivienne's free hand traveled up his back, ruffled his hair, and pulled his mouth down to hers. But it made clear what her idea was.

Still nuzzling each other—even at that instant he could admire the skill with which she confronted the cabman with the back of her own head and the mere top of his—they halted. The driver chuckled and pressed the door button.

The woman shoved the generator into the rear and climbed after it. "Really, Tom, I've got to get back to work," she whined. "The boss'll skin me alive as is, because I didn't deliver this test rig to his place yesterday like I was supposed to.''

Koskinen couldn't think of any response. Her fingers pinched him savagely. "Oh!" He entered behind her. "Uh, don't, don't worry about that, uh, sweetheart. I'll see to it that he's, uh, satisfied.''

"Gee, it must be nice to have money," she purred. The door closed behind him. The driver punched for top speed, uppermost Controlled level, and the surge pressed his passengers yet closer together.

He gave her a clumsy bear hug. "Oof," she whispered. "Easy, there, bruiser." His nostrils filled with the warm odors of her, hair that smelled like sunshine and skin like—he had no comparisons. The heart racketed in him and he must force breath past the fullness in his throat.

From the corner of an eye, without much interest, Koskinen glimpsed the rising sun. In that light megalopolis became a romantic, tower-pierced mist-land, where the two rivers and Long Island Sound lay like molten silver. There were not many other cars to be seen. The taxi fled eastward, faster than he wished. Before long the city gave way to garden-scape rolling back from wide beaches, only an occasional Center breaking its serenity. When this area was rebuilt, none but the wealthiest could afford to live there, and they did not let industry return.

The bulk of Centralia marched over the horizon. "What flange, sir?" asked the driver. He had to repeat himself twice before Koskinen heard, checked his memory, and stammered, "T-T twenty-third. West side, that is."

"Very good, sir." The driver called ahead for permission from the chief of guard. It was granted without fuss; taxis came here often enough. He slanted his vehicle downward, touched wheels to flexiplast, and let the machine proceed under ground guidance to a disembarkation ramp.

Vivienne had already slipped money into Koskinen's pocket. "Give him a fat tip," she breathed tenderly in his ear. Still dazed, aware mostly of her, he nodded. "Oh, my," she laughed, "I must look like a perfect mutie."

"You look beautiful," he faltered.

She took the generator and went out. He paid off the cabman, who winked and muttered, "You're a lucky one today, aren't you?" his eyes on Vivienne's provocatively retreating back rather than Koskinen's undistinguished face. The taxi threaded its way among the several private cars parked on the flange, bounced aloft, and headed toward Manhattan.

Koskinen followed the woman up the ramp to a terrace. There brooklets tinkled through beds of moss and banks of rosebushes, wet with dew. Vivienne had paused beneath the pale red fire of a flowering plum tree. She was looking across the gardens below, to the dazzling beach and breakers, water that glittered green and gulls that wheeled snow-colored in the wind.

He ventured to lay an arm around her waist. She sighed and leaned her head against his shoulder. "I'd almost forgotten how lovely Earth can be," she murmured.

"I've just started to learn . . . from you," he surprised himself by answering.

She chuckled. "You learn pretty quick, Pete, I must say."

A footfall scrunched on gravel. They turned, instantly alert. There had been no attendants on the landing flange, but the man in the control tower had evidently noticed strangers getting off and suggested that the guards check on them. The man who neared wore no uniform—in this stratum of society there was no need for ostentation—and he walked leisurely, with a smile on his mouth. But Koskinen recognized trained muscles when he saw them in motion; and there was a minicom on the wrist.

"Good morning, sir," he hailed. "Can I be of service?"

"Yes," Koskinen said. "I'd like to see Mr. Abrams."

"Sir?" The guard raised skeptical brows.

"My name is Koskinen. I was a shipmate of David Abrams, and I've got some news that will interest his father."

Professional calm broke in an oath not quite suppressed. "Of course, Mr. Koskinen! Right away! He's still asleep, I think, but—— Follow me, please."

Koskinen took the generator from Vivienne and slung it on his shoulder by one strap. She tugged at his hand, holding him back, as the guard started away. He saw the tension in her, and realized with a sudden hollowness that she had stopped thinking about the taxi ride.

"What's going on, Pete?" she whispered unsteadily. "I've heard of Nathan Abrams. Isn't he a big man in General Atomics? What are you coming to him for?"

"Don't you remember that MS has got his son incommunicado? I think he'll be more than glad to help us. We have a common cause."

"You idiot!" she exploded under her breath. "Don't you think MS knows that too?"

"Oh, yes. Doubtless they've had him under surveillance. It was a risk coming here. But not too big a risk. They can't watch everything, especially right now when their hands must be full cleaning out the Chinese organization that tipped its hand

99

at the Crater. Because we did escape, you see, and so the Chinese couldn't have made a fast getaway of their own, they must have lost time searching that warren for us, and that would have given MS time to learn about the affair and intervene. Only MS would've had to pull in every local agent, I should think, on such short notice. I'm quite sure there's no stakeout here at the moment."

"Unless MS has agents in the household."

"I doubt that too. Dave often told me that his father had spent years building up a staff loyal to him personally. All the big executives do. It's necessary, in this wolf kennel world we've got."

"M-m . . . well . . . the fact that we haven't yet been nabbed does seem to bear out your reasoning." She looked at him so searchingly that his own eyes must drop. "Good work. A professional couldn't have thought faster on his feet. You know, kid, you catch on to things so quickly that it scares me. But come on, the guard's waiting for us."

They were conducted through a sliding vitryl door into the building. A fountain splashed twenty feet high in the middle of the solarium beyond. Koskinen saw that its starkly beautiful basin had been fashioned from a spaceship's meteorite baffle. The pouring water, the brilliant morning light, the smell of lilies growing in beds on the flagged floor, brought the whole great room alive. But his attention focused on the man who hurried to meet them.

It was not the elder Abrams, but a stocky, grizzled person, dressed in a plain blue zipsuit, whom the guard addressed deferentially. After a moment's conference, the newcomer dismissed the other man and approached. His face was older than his athletic gait, with skin drawn tight over broad cheekbones and beaky nose but deeply lined around mouth and eyes. Koskinen had seldom met so intense a gaze. The handclasp was hard. He introduced himself and Vivienne.

"I'm Jan Trembecki, Mr. Abrams's confidential secretary. He'll be along in a few minutes. Won't you sit down?" The English was fluent but accented.

"Thanks." Koskinen began to realize how tired he was. He nearly fell into a lounger and let it mold itself to hips and ribs. Vivienne lowered herself more gracefully, but shivering with exhaustion. Trembecki considered them. "How about some breakfast?" he asked, punched an intercom button and spoke an order.

Returning, he offered cigarettes. Vivienne accepted, drawing the smoke far into her lungs and letting it out as if reluctantly. Trembecki sat on the edge of a lounger and puffed his own cigarette in short ferocious drags.

"I take it you escaped from MS," he said. When Koskinen nodded; "Well, we may be able to hide you—or we may not—but let's be blunt. Why should we? We've got troubles enough."

"I may have help for you," Koskinen answered. He pointed to the generator. "That's the reason for this whole mess."

"Ah, so." Trembecki grew altogether expressionless. "We've had some inklings of that, from our own efforts to investigate."

"Do you think Dave is . . . all right?"

"I don't expect anything permanently damaging has been done to him. Doubtless he's been PI'd, but if he doesn't have any special knowledge—does he?" The question spat like a bullet. Koskinen started before he shook his head. "Good. In that case, Dave is mainly a sort of hostage. Therefore he has to be preserved intact. To be sure, that ties our own hands quite a bit."

"What have you been trying to do? Couldn't you——Mr. Abrams should be able to, oh, even get the President's ear."

"He will, in due course. That takes time, though, no matter how prominent one is. Especially since the President's staff can find ways to stall if they're put to it. And they no doubt have been. Every government employee is terrified of MS; a bad report can cost you your job, or worse, in Washington."

"But the President himself——"

"Yes, we're lucky there. He's a libertarian by conviction. However, he's responsible for the security of the United States, which nowadays means the stability of the Protectorate. MS is indispensable to that. So Marcus can get away with almost anything."

"But the President can fire Marcus!"

"Things aren't that simple, my friend. You have to respect the integrity of a government organization, or you'll soon have no government whatsoever. Furthermore, every leader has to make compromises; otherwise he'd set everybody against him and get nothing accomplished. Read some history. Consider how Lincoln had to put up with all the foolishness in his Cabinet, not to mention a fantastic series of leatherheaded commanding generals. Or the uneasy balance between Stalinists and anti-Stalinists in the old Soviet Union. Or—— never mind. It boils down to the fact that the President can't fire Marcus unless extreme wrongdoing can be proven, and can't countermand any orders given MS unless he *and* Congress are convinced the orders were utterly mistaken.''

"Maybe we can convince him," Koskinen said.

"Maybe. Hard to do through legal, public channels, though. And if we commit illegalities ourselves—like sheltering a fugitive from, shall we say, justice—we compromise our case rather badly.''

Koskinen let his muscles slump. For a while only the fountain spoke.

"Ah, refreshments.''

Koskinen opened his eyes with a shocked realization that he had been asleep. A servitor halted and uncovered its table. Koskinen looked at coffee, orange juice, French rolls, butter, cheese, caviar, an iced bottle of vodka. Trembecki handed him and Vivienne a couple of stimpills. "Better take these first," he suggested. "You'll enjoy the food more.''

"Also," Vivienne said grimly, "we'll need our brains in good shape.''

They had hardly begun when two figures appeared in the inner entrance. Trembecki rose. "Sorry to postpone your breakfast," he said, "but here's the boss.''

XI

NATHAN ABRAMS was not a tall man, and he was getting somewhat bald and plump. The bathrobe swirled almost ludicrously about his pajamaed legs as he turned in his pacing. But Koskinen had never before seen so great an anger on so tight a leash.

A little hoarse with talking, he sat back and listened to his host. "Good Lord," Abrams said through his teeth, "I had some notion of how much rottenness there is around, but when the thing comes out in the open like this, it's past time to fight!"

"Using what for weapons?" Trembecki asked.

Abrams's hand chopped in the direction of the shield unit. "There's that, to start with."

"Take quite a while to produce enough and organize a group."

"And meanwhile Dave——". Leah Abrams's voice wavered. As if to give herself something to do, she began putting food on the plates. "I'm

104

sorry," she said to Koskinen and Vivienne. "You must be starved."

In spite of everything, Koskinen's look and mind turned to her. He had naturally known about Dave's sister, but she was only fifteen when the *Boas* departed. He had not expected to find someone slim and supple, gray eyes, freckles dusted faintly across a piquant nose, reddish-brown hair falling softly to her shoulders, a dancer's way of walking. She must have considerable backbone too, he thought. Abrams had not yet told his wife about this meeting, he didn't know if she could stand it, but his daughter had come along as a matter of course.

Besides, it was good of her to remember about breakfast. He *was* starved. Still he hesitated, while Abrams stood and fought himself. The girl seemed to read his thought. "Go ahead," she urged. "You needn't pretend that our troubles have spoiled your appetite. As a matter of fact, I think I'll have a bite myself."

Vivienne smiled. "You're too tactful for your own good. But thanks, Miss Abrams."

"Leah, if you don't mind. We're in the same army now."

"I'm not so sure of that," Trembecki said.

"What do you mean, Jan?" Abrams demanded.

"Well——"

"I wasn't proposing anything rash, you know. We want Dave back first of all, and everyone else from the ship. We've got to proceed cautiously. But sooner or later, maybe we'll have to——" Abrams broke off.

Trembecki finished for him in a brutal tone: "Fight against our own government?"

"Well . . . against Marcus, at least. This puts the capper on everything I'd known about the man previously. I tell you, he's a power maniac, and he's got to be stopped."

"Let's drop the swear words, Nat," Trembecki said. "Neo-fascism doesn't come out of nowhere, any more than Caesarism does. That's what we've got now, Caesarism, modified only slightly by the fact that it arose in a republic more sophisticated than Rome was. But it arose as the answer to a very real need, survival in the thermonuclear age. You don't want to overthrow Caesar if the price is a civil war that weakens us for the barbarians."

"I wasn't thinking of any such nonsense!"

"It was implicit, though, Nat. In a subtler form, perhaps: less an outright revolt than a disruption of a precarious balance of social forces. Which could mean economic chaos. When that happens—when a society fails to provide for its own internal needs—the way is open for total dictatorship. The popular will demands a strong man then. Freedom isn't worth seeing your children starve. Not to most people, anyhow.

"Marcus has millions of admirers precisely because you and your kind have failed to solve problems like foreign enmity, overpopulation, maldistribution, educational lag, and social vacuums. If now the American upper classes fall out among themselves, with even the mildest analogue of the Marius-Sulla rivalry, the failure will grow worse yet. Maybe Marcus could be destroyed, but he'd have successors who'd destroy us in turn. No, quite apart from all the practical difficulties in the way of our doing something big and melodramatic, we've got responsibilities that won't let us."

"You weren't so shy about consequences when you helped take Krakow from that warlord," Abrams said bitterly.

"I was a good deal younger then," Trembecki sighed, "and in any case the issues were simpler."

Leah leaned over and whispered to Koskinen and Vivienne: "He's from Central Europe, did you know? Dad found him running a city in Poland and persuaded him to come work in the States."

Koskinen regarded Trembecki with increased respect. The war and postwar years had been bad enough in America. But at least no foreign troops had invaded, to run amok and add to the chaos after the missiles destroyed their homeland. If, besides surviving and restoring order, this man had found time to become educated——

"Don't get me wrong," Trembecki said. "I don't propose tamely to turn over this thing for Marcus to slap a 'security' label on and find ways to misuse. Frankly, I don't know how far we ourselves can be trusted with it. You're a decent man, Nat, and I suppose I am, but General Atomics isn't our private empire. With the best intentions in the world, given this kind of power, it could become something it shouldn't be.

"Leaving that aside, though, you're disqualified from doing much precisely because you are so influential. Your actions are all too public for you to get involved in any elaborate conspiracy.

You're simply going to have to stick to the aboveboard approach. Whatever you do clandestinely has to be a very, very minor part of your total activity, and amount to little more than keeping in touch with whoever is being active.''

"Ah-ha," Abrams pounced. "You admit there has to be a conspiracy."

"No. Maybe there does. Maybe not. This has happened so fast. I haven't had time to think."

"You won't get much time, either," Vivienne reminded him bleakly.

"With Marcus on the trail . . . true," the Pole nodded. "I don't see how we can hide you for any great length of time. However big a household this is, it's still not an organization. And that's what you need, an organization with intelligence agents, hideouts, an Underground Railway—yet one that can be trusted."

Abrams snapped his fingers. "The Egalitarians!"

"Hm?" Trembecki gave him a startled look. "You mean Gannoway?"

"I don't know. But we can check on him, maybe."

"I'm not sure what you mean," Leah said, "but if it has anything to do with the Egalitarians, why, it sounds very hopeful. I've been to plenty of their meetings, and talked to a lot of them, you know. Dad, those are *good* people."

"Perhaps," Trembecki grunted. "Are they effective people, though?"

"Gannoway himself is a tough bird," Abrams mused, "still . . . we may have something here.

It's taking a devil of a risk at best, but——"
ruefully——"what isn't?"

Trembecki nodded with a renewed briskness.
"I'll start some wheels turning, at least. We'll
collect what information we can, evaluate, and
decide what to do. It should be safe to keep our
young friends here for a little while. The sooner
we get them to a really secure place, though, the
happier I'll be."

"All right. Let's get started." Abrams turned to
Koskinen and Vivienne. "I'm sorry to rush off
like this, but you can understand why. We'll talk
in more detail later. Meanwhile, Leah will take
care of you."

Trembecki went over to the shield generator,
which Koskinen had demonstrated in the course of
relating his story. The secretary picked it up with
needless care, held it for a space before his eyes,
clicked his tongue, and walked from the room.
Abrams followed.

"Do finish eating," Leah urged. "I'll see about
your rooms and stuff. Be right back."

Koskinen fell heartily to eating. In combina-
tion, the stimulant, food, shelter, sense of power
and competence in those he met, had restored him
considerable cheer. "I think," he said around a
mouthful, "we're on the homestretch."

"Really?" Vivienne only picked at her meal. He
saw the exhaustion still in her and wanted to
soothe it away. But his tongue knotted.

"Sorry," she said after a while. "I guess I've
been kicked around too much to start believing in
Santa Claus all over again."

"If Papa Abrams put on a white beard and went, 'Ho, ho, ho!' would that help?" he ventured.

She grinned wearily, leaned over and patted his hand. "You mean you've even got patience with self-pity? You're a phenomenon, Pete."

Leah's footsteps sounded lightly on the flags. Koskinen rose and looked at the girl as she neared. He wondered confusedly if it was right to be so conscious of her grace, so soon after——

"Finished here?" she asked. "Good, come along with me. You'll want to wash and then sleep, I suppose."

"Not sleep," Koskinen said, "with fifty milligrams of stim inside me."

"I'd forgotten that. Well, if you like, I'll be glad to give you the grand tour of the place, or any other entertainment I can."

"You're being too kind."

Leah grew grave. "You were Dave's shipmate, Pete. He talked a lot about you, in the short time he was here. And you've done some magnificent things, for him and for all of us."

"No, really."

"Not just that filthy Crater, but perhaps even the Chinese underground, wiped out . . . because of you." The long hair swirled past her cheeks as she shook her head in wonder. "I still can't quite believe it."

"That was an accident. I mean, I was only running away, and——"

"Come on." She took him firmly by the arm. Vivienne followed a little behind, silent.

A glideway and escalator took them upstairs.

Koskinen had thought his hotel room and Vivienne's Crater place were sumptuous, but his suite here revised his standards. He pottered about for half an hour making himself presentable. In the course of undressing he noticed the chain still around his neck. *Have to get that taken off*, he thought, but forgot about it again.

Putting on a lounge suit that felt almost as silky as a Martian cloakleaf, he returned to Leah in the solarium. "Come outside till Vivienne arrives," she suggested. "It's such a gorgeous day."

They strolled over the terrace to the parapet. Leah leaned against it and gazed out across the Sound. A breeze fluttered her hair and shook a few plum blossoms down over her. *Vee has paused at this same spot*, Koskinen remembered.

He drew a lungful of untainted air. "You're right about the outdoors today," he remarked. "Sometimes that seemed to be what we missed the most on Mars. Earth's weather, every kind of it."

"But they have weather there too, don't they?"

"Yes. Nothing like ours, though. Days so clear that space itself didn't seem to exist between you and the horizon, then night falling at once, no dusk, just suddenly the stars appearing like fireworks, and so cold you could hear the rocks groan as they contracted. Or a dust storm, thin enough for the sunlight to shine through, making diamond sparkles across those old, old crags. Or the spring quickening, when the polar cap melted and the bands of forest came to life again, those grotesque little trees raising their tendrils toward the sun and unfolding yard-long leaves that took on a hundred different colors, greens, russets, golds, blues, and danced as if for joy——'' Koskinen shook himself. "Excuse me. For a minute if almost seemed as if I were back there."

"Would you want to return, ever?" she asked quietly.

"Yes. Eventually. We got to be good friends with the Martians, you know."

"Dave said a little about that too. Is 'friends' really the word you want?"

"No. There was something between all of us, the whole crew as well as the Martians. Affection was a major part of it, but somehow so transformed that——I don't know. You'd have to experience it yourself to have any idea of what I mean. Now that I've been away from it for a while, I have some trouble understanding the concept myself."

"I'd like to try," she said.

"You ought to," he said, caught in a sudden uprush of enthusiasm. "There definitely should be women on the next expedition. We could only realize an incomplete rapport, because we ourselves were incomplete. It'll take the full human unit, man-woman-child, to . . . to establish a total relationship with the Martians. You see, they don't communicate just with verbal language. We've got plenty of non-verbal communication on Earth, of course, but very little of it has been systematized or developed. What's a synonym for a grimace? How do you conjugate a wave of your hand? I'm putting it horribly crudely, of course; but what I'm trying to get at is that the Martians look on communication as a function of the whole organism. They have a complete tactile language, for instance, as well as a verbal one, a musical one, a choreographic one, and lots more. And those languages are not equivalent to each other, the way writing is equivalent to speech. They don't say the same things, they don't cover the same range of possible subject matter. But when you use several of them simultaneously . . . can you imagine how complete a view of reality might be approached?

"Only, for that kind of communication there has to be a psychological affinity, a oneness, between the communicators, because it's so subtle a process. I think we humans learned as much as we could have digested in five years anyway. But next time we ought to go further. And that gets back to the necessity of completing ourselves. I mean by bringing both sexes there, and every age, race, culture we can get."

"You know," she said, "I begin to see why Dave liked . . . likes you so much. You're a completely unstuffy idealist."

He glanced away in confusion. "I didn't mean to preach."

"I wish you would," she said. "I want so much to get an idea of what it was like on Mars, what you did and discovered and thought, everything. After all, Dave was there, and we hardly had a chance to get to know him again before—— But for its own sake too, I'd like to know. And someday go there myself. Actually, didn't the experience of the rapport mean more to you than anything you learned from it?" He nodded, astonished at her quick perceptiveness. "Well, I wish for that experience too," she said. "You've already given me back the wonder in life. People have gotten so blasé about spaceships and orbital stations and extra-terrestrial bases that I'd forgotten what it really means. But now I'll see Mars in the sky and think, 'That little red spark is a *world*,' and feel a chill down my spine. Suddenly the limits have been taken away. Thanks for that, Pete.''

It puzzled him how they had begun talking so intimately so soon. *I guess it's that we're in a stress situation and our personal barriers are down,* he decided. *And Dave belongs to us both. She's a lot like him, whom I've come to know as well as I know myself. Not too much like him, though*, he added sophomorically. Then he forgot the matter. It was trivial beside that with which they spent the better part of the day.

Late in the afternoon Leah came to herself with a shaky laugh. ''You've got to excuse me, Pete. I'm on the local committee for the World War One Centennial observances. We're going to re-enact a Liberty Bond rally, if that means anything to you. The whole business looks more foolish than ever, after what you and I have been talking about. But I don't dare do anything unusual, like cutting out of the meeting. Not now.''

He agreed, thrown unwillingly back to the immediacies, and moped about the place after she was gone. Finally he drifted into an imperial-sized library. A book would at least kill time.

Vivienne sat there reading. She wore a white dress, reminding him of the night she entertained him, and he wondered in a stunned fashion how he could have forgotten about her.

"Oh," she said in a lackluster tone. "Hello, there."

"Why didn't you join us?" he asked. "When you didn't show, we figured you'd decided to sleep instead."

"No. I came out on the terrace," she shrugged. "But you were so deep in conversation I didn't want to butt in."

"Vee! We weren't discussing any . . . any secrets. How could we have been?"

Her lips twitched ever so faintly upward. "Now why did you suppose I'd think that? Of course you weren't."

"Then why didn't you——"

The smile ceased to be. She looked away from him. "I know when I'm out of my class," she said, "and frankly, I've got too much pride to play-act at the case being otherwise."

"What are you talking about?" he protested. "Brains? Good Lord, Vee, you can think rings around ninety percent of the human race."

"Probably. Brains is not what I meant." Her tone grew jagged. "Look, Pete, I'm not mad at you or anything, but will you please get out of here for a while? And close the door when you go."

XII

KOSKINEN returned the following afternoon from a violent game of handball with Leah—he dared not show himself outside the residence, but it included a gymnasium—to be informed by a servant of a conference at 1600. They changed clothes and went to the study at that hour. Vivienne and Trembecki had already joined Abrams there.

The executive gave his daughter an unhappy look. "Not you, my dear," he said.

"Don't be silly, Dad," she protested. "I'm in this as much as anybody."

"Yes, and I wish you weren't. We're not playing tiddlywinks."

"I found out the hard way in Europe," Trembecki added, "that the fewer people who have complete knowledge of an operation like this, the better."

"I wouldn't blab," she said indignantly.

"Of course not. But there are such things as PI drugs."

"Do you mean somebody might kidnap me?"

"No. It's sufficient if they arrest you, just as they did Dave."

"Oh." She bit her lip. "Yes. What can I do, then, to help?"

"The hardest thing of all: sit tight."

"Well——" She squared her shoulders. "I'll be seeing you, Pete. I mean that." Her hand lingered in his for a moment before she went out. The door slid to behind her like a closing mouth.

"For the same reason," Trembecki said, "I think we'd better leave that bomb around your neck."

Vivienne stirred uneasily in her chair. One hand went to a small purse clipped on her belt. Slowly she relaxed again. "Maybe," she said, flat-voiced.

"You're the logical person to keep the detonator," Trembecki said to her. "You don't know how to make a shield unit yourself, do you?"

"No. We didn't finish drawing the plans in the Crater, and without a background of theory, what circuits I can remember are just so much junk."

"That leaves you the only person who does know, Pete." Abrams's regard of Koskinen was troubled. "Do you agree——if worst comes to worst, Vivienne should be able to silence you? Life as a permanent prisoner wouldn't be fun anyway."

"I guess so," Koskinen dragged out of himself.

"Not that I expect any such outcome," Abrams said less glumly. "In fact, things are looking up for us. Sit down and let's talk over our next move." He placed himself behind his desk, bridged his fingers, and considered for a space before he started:

"Our problem, as I see it, is this. We've got to keep the shield from falling into the wrong hands, yet use it as a bargaining counter to get our friends released and, if possible, to get Marcus out of office. The best way to work is through the President. If he can be convinced of the truth, and I think he can, he will act. After all, once the United States armed forces have shields—most especially, once our cities and other vulnerable points do— then the Protectorate won't need very tight controls over the rest of the world. If MS can't actually be abolished, it can at least be sharply reduced in size and function. That will please the libertarians and the economy-minded in Congress, without offending too much those who make a fetish of national security.

"But it'll take time for me to get an appointment; and then a single talk won't accomplish much. All I can hope to do the first time is get him so interested that he'll agree to let you demonstrate the effect. That will have to be done secretly, so Marcus can't forestall us. I wouldn't put it past him to have you assassinated and the generator destroyed, if there's no other way to safeguard his power. Such a meeting between you and the President obviously requires careful prearrangement. And then still more time must pass while the President sets the political stage for what will almost be a *coup d'état* in legal form. In the meantime, you'll need a safe hiding place.

"Jan could have arranged that easily in his old days. But unfortunately, he and I have lived blameless lives for many years now. We haven't got the right kind of contacts. I trust the loyalty of the household staff, but not their ability to play tag with the cops. Given a week or so, we could doubtless arrange a good bolthole for you; but we don't have that week. You mustn't stay here an hour longer than necessary. Your guess was right about MS, my Washington sources tell me. They did pick up so many leads and clues about the Chinese underground that it's taken almost all their resources to follow through. But their attention is sure to turn back on me good and hard as soon as that pressure eases off, which I imagine won't be long now.

"So . . . it is a risk, but I think the least risk we can get by with, if we try turning you over to the Equals."

"Who are they?" Koskinen asked. "It seems I've heard mention of some such name, but I don't place it."

"Short for Egalitarians. They're an idealistic movement, a number of people who want the Protectorate converted into a representative world government. That in itself isn't an illegal thing to advocate. Sure, Marcus and men of his stripe have denounced them as softheads and stooges for foreign interests. But nothing has been done about them because there's nothing that needs to be done. They only organize clubs, discuss, propagandize, work in election years for candidates sympathetic to their ideas. They're mainly significant because they attract a lot of intellectuals."

"They don't sound very promising for our purposes," Vivienne said. "In fact, those Equals I've met in the past tended to be dear old ladies . . . of both sexes."

Abrams laughed. "True. Not all, however. There seem to be some Equals who believe in direct action. And they don't tell the dear old ladies about that."

"What sort of action?"

"If I'd been able to find out in detail, the group wouldn't be worth much. The fact is, though, that outlawed books and pamphlets get published and circulated, calling for violent overthrow of agencies like MS. More significantly, people sometimes disappear when they get in trouble with the Protectorate. Remember Yamashita a few years ago? He was stirring up the Japanese people on quite a large scale—if stirring up is the right word; actually he preached passive resistance. MS arrested him, then lost him again. They haven't caught him yet. But he keeps popping up in remote villages, still drawing crowds to hear him, and vanishes before MS can arrive. There are several similar cases known to me, and doubtless many that I haven't heard of. Well, this sort of thing takes organization. *Somebody* is operating an underground which isn't nationalistic but universalistic. I suspect very strongly that Equals are involved. They may well be the prime movers."

"I don't like it," Trembecki muttered. "I think the outfit has engineered some murders too."

"Maybe. But the victims needed murdering. Like General Friedmann. Remember what he did to stop the protest marches in Rome?"

"Um-m-m. . . . Granted, I'm not one to talk about niceties. And anyway, I haven't a better suggestion to make. Go on, Nat."

"So," Abrams said, "there's this Carson Gannoway, executive secretary of the local chapter of the computermen's union, and an Egalitarian. I've dealt with him for years, and in the past couple of days I've had my personal detective staff investigate him to within an inch of his life. He's not overtly involved with the underground, of course, but I've gotten some strong hints. For instance, there've been illegal strikes now and then, with some violence. Gannoway, like the rest of his union's officials, publicly deplored them, asked the men to go back to work, and said he was helpless against their 'spontaneous action.' But, while conspiracy could never be proved, someone had obviously put them up to those walkouts. Now I know Gannoway and I know that he could have prevented or aborted those affairs if he'd really wanted. He's that able. Which suggests he was the actual brains behind them. Or there's the fact that he's been gone on 'vacation' several times precisely when something broke . . . like when the Toronto rioters suddenly acquired guns."

"Has MS noticed him?" Vivienne asked.

"No, not particularly, I'm sure. They can't keep tabs on every last one of us, thank God, and Gannoway isn't a conspicuous public figure. It's only because I, as I said, have known him so long, that I slowly got the idea he had connections with the underground. I wasn't about to rat on him. I haven't been violently anti-Marcus until now, but

I never liked the way MS operates. Why shouldn't somebody like Yamashita remind his people that they have a heritage of their own? So I simply kept my suspicions to myself. The underground never did me any harm. Now maybe it can help us.''

"You think, then, Gannoway can——'' Koskinen choked on his own excitement.

"Well, we'll try him and see,'' Abrams said. "Jan phoned him today and asked if he could drop around to his home tonight to discuss a business matter. You two will go along. If he can hide you, great. If not, I'm sure he'll keep his mouth shut. Then we'll arrange a place for you in a warehouse I know of, though it'll be a poor substitute.''

"If he does offer to hide us, but I don't like the looks of the offer, we'll head straight back too,'' Trembecki said.

"Us?'' Vivienne said. "You're going to be with Pete and me?''

The Pole nodded. "I'm still tolerably fast with a spitgun,'' he said, touching a spot beneath his tunic. "Though what I really want is to—— Well, Vee, you can land on your feet as reliably as the next she-tiger, but Pete here seems, frankly, a wee bit naive. I think he could use a word on occasion, from a guy who's had some experience with the underside of the world.''

XIII

GANNOWAY'S home was a modest apartment in Queens, crowded by a wife and four children. But he had a study of his own which he assured his visitors was soundproof and free of electronic bugs; and his family had been sent out for the evening.

A tall, angular, somewhat Andrew Jackson-featured man, he closed the study door and stood considering the others. Koskinen shifted from foot to foot under that gaze, glanced out the window at the glittering sprawl of the night city, back again to the comfort of Vivienne beside him, and did not know what to say. When Gannoway broke the silence, it was Trembecki he addressed.

"You must have some reason for bringing me these outlaws, Jan, and you're not the type to try to frame me. But I'd appreciate it if you'd end the suspense."

"Outlaws?" Vivienne exclaimed. "Has the alarm been 'cast?"

"Yeah, an hour or so ago," Gannoway said.

"On the evening news. Names and photos, with a tape excerpt from Mr. Koskinen's last phone call to the Bureau. You're dangerous foreign agents, did you know?"

"Damn! I'd hoped for a little more time," Trembecki said. "But evidently the Chinese job is completed. They'll be after you now in full force, Pete."

"What does MS really want you for?" Gannoway asked.

"That's a long story," Trembecki said. "You'll hear it *if*."

"I knew the Mars expedition had been taken into 'protective custody,' of course, and wondered why. I'm sorry about Nat's boy."

"Part of getting him back is to keep these kids free," Trembecki said. "We have to hide them away for a period of time, a month or longer. You know every place Nat's got will be checked, just because Dave's arrest has made him a natural ally of theirs. Can you take care of them?"

"Here? Don't make me laugh. And while I sympathize with anybody in that position, why should I jeopardize my family, as well as myself, on your account?"

"On your own account too," Trembecki said. "Wouldn't you like to get rid of Marcus? Pete, here, has a way to do so, if we can apply it."

Gannoway's features remained immobile, but the breath sucked sharply in between his lips. "Sit down and tell me."

"I'm afraid you'll have to take my word," Trembecki answered. "We've had our differences now and then, you and Nat and I, but you know we aren't doublecrossers.''

Gannoway shook his head. "Sorry. Your judgment of what's right and proper might not square with mine. Besides, I couldn't do a thing by myself. Others would be involved, who do not know you personally. They'd have to be convinced the risk was worth taking.''

"And that they'd have some say in the final settlement?''

"Well . . . yes. If you've got, let's suppose, a gadget potent enough to overthrow Marcus and keep someone equally bad from succeeding him——'' Gannoway gestured at the shield generator by Koskinen's feet——"then it's probably also able to accomplish other things.''

"The possibilities are big, all right,'' Trembecki said. "We wouldn't have turned to you if there'd been much choice in the matter. Nothing personal, Carse, but how far can we trust your associates?''

"All the way, provided you want the same as they do.''

"Which is what?''

"Read Quarles and find out. We're simply followers of his.''

"So you say. But he wouldn't be the first prophet in history whose teachings got twisted.''

"He's still alive, you know, to keep us in line,'' Gannoway said. "Professor emeritus at Columbia. I see him quite often.''

He sat brooding before he addressed Koskinen: "Look here, if you're the one that this hullaballoo is about, you're entitled to the deciding vote.

What do you think? Will you trust me without reservations, or would you rather go off and forget you ever saw me? In the latter case, I won't fink on you, even though I'll be in serious trouble if you're caught and PI'd. But I hope you'll choose the first.''

"I——" Koskinen moistened his lips. "I don't . . . that is, I'm so ignorant about everything on Earth, I can't——"

Vivienne reached over to lay a hand on his. "He's had a nasty time," she said. "How's he to know who his friends are?"

"We can't sit long and argue," Gannoway warned. "But . . . wait, I have a suggestion. Why not invite Quarles over so you can find out what Egalitarianism really is, and decide if it's something you can honestly support?"

"Hey, we don't want to let anyone else in on the fact that these people are with us," Trembecki said.

"No problem there," Gannoway assured him. "He's been blind for years. We'll simply introduce you under different names."

"Would he come over, just like that?" Koskinen asked.

"Probably. He's alone in the world. I've had him here often for an evening's chat."

"I've been party to some strange negotiations," Trembecki grumbled, "but making a lecture on sociology a beforehand requirement takes the pink sugar cake."

"No. I think Mr. Gannoway's right," Koskinen said. "I, that is, maybe it's hard for you to understand, but we'd have done this sort of thing on

Mars, trying to get the wholeness of a situation. I mean, well, emotion is the largest part of it, and that's not something you can put in a book like logic. It's something that someone is feeling here-and-now. You have to encounter it directly."

"I'll call, then." Gannoway left the room.

Trembecki shook his head. "I wish I'd had more to do with the Equals," he muttered. "I'd have some notion, then, of the ins and outs of them, even their clandestine fraction. As matters are, I can only go by guess and feel. Might be a good idea to talk to the old man at that. Of course, he probably has no idea that an underground exists, but sometimes you can judge a tree by its roots." He lit a cigarette and let it droop from his mouth. "Sometimes."

Gannoway came back. "Everything's fine. He'll take a cab right away. I told him I had some people visiting, fresh from several years of engineering work abroad, who'd love to meet him." He chuckled. "Oren Quarles is a saint, I suppose, but he has his human share of vanity."

"Let's get our yarns straight," Trembecki said. "Aliases and such details." They spent the interval of waiting in rehearsal. When Quarles arrived, they moved out to the living room.

The philosopher was a small man, but carried himself so erect that one scarcely noticed. A massive white-thatched head was framed in the thin cage of a "seeing eye," whose reflected pulses enabled him to find his way around with fair ease. There was courtliness in the manner with which he shook hands, bowing over Vivienne's, and accepted a glass of sherry. A while passed in the usual polite formulas. But he was not hard to steer onto the subject of his own ideas.

"To be frank," he said, "I don't like that name 'Egalitarianism.' For one thing, it's uneuphonious —or should I say dysphonious?—and for another, it fixes a label. People are much too apt to identify the label with the bottle, no matter how much the contents may change. Look at what happened to concepts like Christianity and democracy.

"The latter is particularly relevant. Democracy came to be identified with freedom. That ain't necessarily so, as de Tocqueville realized, and Jouvenel after him. If the popular will prevails unrestrained, then there is nothing government cannot do, and hence no limit to the degree of control which it can impose on the individual. Louis XIV daydreamed about conscription, but only the French Revolutionary government was actually able to institute it. Or, on a more mundane level, democratic communities tend to have a set of blue laws such as would never be imagined in an aristocracy or a monarchy. I really believe that the present-day liberalism about public morals and display—anything goes, they tell me, and what's still technically illegal is winked at—I really think that stems directly from the decline of democracy: if only because it helps hide the more important freedoms which have been lost."

"But we have a democracy still," Koskinen blurted. "Don't we?"

"In a way. We still elect our legislators and our principal executives. However, the percentage of the population that bothers to vote grows smaller every year. And that isn't merely the result of poverty, poor education, and the rest, bad though things are in those regards. It reflects a general realization that the true government has become a set of bureaus: inevitably so, given the requirements of world empire. And these bureaus, in turn, are gradually becoming the private fiefs of those men strong and clever enough to get control of their machinery. Military Security is the most conspicuous example, but the others aren't far behind in that line of evolution. If you want to do something in industry, science, communications, almost anything you care to name, you hardly ever deal with a Senator or a Congressman, trying to get laws passed that will favor you. Do you? No, you approach an agency in charge of administering and interpreting laws already passed.''

"Do you mean Congress is a rubber stamp?'' Koskinen asked.

"Not yet. The final authority is still there, if Congress can be induced to use it. But that would require the repeal of a century's legislation, all of which involved giving government more and more scope and, therefore, giving those who execute that legislation more and more power. This in turn derives from the basis on which democratic government claims legitimacy: the naked popular will. (Which, in practice, means the will of the most effective pressure groups.) The Founding Fathers were well aware of that tendency, and wrote restrictions into the Constitution, things that government could not do no matter how large a majority wished them done. Actually, this country began as a republic, not a pure democracy. But with the passage of time, many of those guarantees were re-interpreted almost out of existence. The states could no longer control their own internal policies, the individual could no longer bear arms . . . oh, everything happened from the best of motives, with the aim of correcting gross abuses, but the end result was the conversion of the republic to a curious cross between a democracy and an oligarchy. The evolution continues today, with the oligarchic element steadily gaining strength while the democratic one weakens.''

"I thought you favored world democracy," Vivienne said, "but now you speak as if you don't think it's even a good idea for us."

"Oh, on the contrary, my dear. . . . I think the concept of *liberty* is one of the noblest and most ennobling which the mind of man has ever brought forth. But it is not identical with democracy, which is only one form of government.

"The problem is how to establish and guarantee liberty. Man is not capable of being an autonomous individual. If he tries to be, the heart goes out of him. He ends as a miserable, ulcer-ridden, futility-haunted nervous wreck. He needs to be part of a whole culture, with duties as well as privileges. But we libertarians feel that that belongingness should come from within, by his own free choice. He should not have to give more than he wishes, provided he does not take more than a share proportionate to his contribution. Then, too, we must face the fact that the poor we always have with us—the unlucky, the handicapped, the oppressed, yes, and their exploiters, who are also unfortunate—and of course there are those who are simply misguided. These must all be taken care of, or society grows sick and at last welcomes the sharp medicine of dictatorship. But the machinery that takes care of them must not grow too restrictive.

"With all its faults, the democratic republic was the best attempt thus far to solve the problem. It provided a governmental framework in which the ballot box was a permanent check on the arrogance of authority. It allowed the will of the majority to be expressed in action. But it also restrained that will, setting up as a moral absolute the rights of the individual and the community, on which no one could encroach for any reason.

"The trouble was that society changed. Transportation and communication improved until every community was the next door neighbor to every other one, and a mobile population felt no deep loyalty to any of them. Freed from local obligations, responsible only for his own well-being, the individual found that no one was responsible for him. He had to turn to government for whatever help he needed. This meant that government became ever larger and more firmly entrenched in every department of life. You can't pass a Bill of Rights and expect it to take care of itself. To endure, it must have deep-rooted institutions to whose existence it is vital. Similarly, states' rights became a farce when the states themselves ceased to be organic communities and became, instead, mere providers of local services—or, in cases like the old segregation laws, mere agents of a petty tyranny whose victims looked to the national government for relief. And, finally, the nuclear wars shattered morale as well as physical plant. The animal wish to survive overrode every traditional concept of international law. So we got the Protectorate: whose yoke will bear more heavily on us than on the client nations, as our society becomes increasingly Byzantine.

"Sometimes, though, good can come of evil. I think we have a chance, at this moment in history, to restore a true democratic republic on a firmer basis than any which has existed in the past. A world basis."

"I beg your pardon," Trembecki said, "but I've seen a fair amount of this planet, and that won't work. Asians, Africans, even most Europeans and Latin Americans, they aren't Yankees. They don't think like you, want what you do, or care about what you think is important. The converse is also true, of course. That's one reason the Protectorate is hated—it forces those peoples, to some extent, into an unnatural mold. You won't make good democrats of them, ever, any more than they'll make a good Moslem or Hindu or something out of you."

Quarles smiled. "There have been occasional startling overnight changes in national character," he said, "But I don't count on any such thing. In fact, I wouldn't want that to happen, the Americanization of the whole Earth. Not only would it impoverish the human race—think of losing all the rich potentialities in other cultures!—but it would make my pet scheme unfeasible."

"Why, I should think it's the only way you'll ever get a real world government," Koskinen said.

"A single world culture, where everybody agrees on at least the essential points."

"No, not really," Quarles said. "At best, if it could happen, such a thing would only invite a repetition of our own recent past, this time on a planetary scale. But if you have, instead, a diversity of communities, each solid enough to survive as a going concern on a basis of equality with the others, while remaining too different from its fellows to merge with them, then would you not have what the United States began as—a genuine federalism?

"And would it not stimulate a revival of liberty? The atomic individual is at the mercy of government because he has no one to stand with him, no community of shared traditions, obligations, folkways. But within the framework of an entire world, a Mexican or Nigerian or Indian would *not* be atomic. He would have just that community, his own nation, whose survival as a distinct entity would require that it be a bulwark against the ex-actions of the central authority. And the same would be true of us Americans."

"What sort of central authority?" Vivienne inquired.

"Well, war has to be prevented. That is the basic necessity, which the Protectorate does serve in its sorry fashion. My own suggestion is that there be a corps of planetary peacekeepers with limited but sufficient powers of inspection and arrest, and a monopoly of the most destructive weapons. (I had to spend an entire chapter defining those!) It should be under the direction of a world president, who's elected by a bicameral world legislature—one Senator from each country and Congressmen according to franchised population.''

"Whoa!" Trembecki exclaimed. "You surely can't mean to give every country equal representation. They tried that in the old UN, with results that you know. And a population basis is every bit as bad. It'd amount to turning the world over to the Chinese."

"I said franchised population," Quarles reminded him. "The requirements for a world-level vote would be such that only the civilized would be included. In fact, I think the multiple ballot is a good idea. Grant an additional world vote for meeting any of several qualifications, such as education above the minimum, real estate ownership, public service, and so on. That would weight the scale still more heavily in favor of reasonable policies. Of course, each country could make what electoral and governmental arrangements it wished within its own borders."

"What else would the world government do?" Koskinen asked.

"Not too much, actually. It could operate in fields like health, conservation, and other politically safe matters. But the principle of internal sovereignty would have to be scrupulously respected. Not that we can continue to let the rich countries get richer while the poor get poorer. There will have to be some way of sharing the economic burden more equally—without merely shielding every community from the consequences of its own mismanagement. I've studied that problem too, in some detail, and concluded that to begin with America could finance an economic program by herself, for approximately what it now costs us to maintain the Protectorate. That would conciliate most of our present enemies, I'm sure. After the first decade, others can begin carrying their share of the load.''

"Too good to be true," Trembecki said. "You can't put countries off in neat little pigeonholes like that. They interact, change, merge, break up. And . . . not every war in history has been unjustified. Deaths, destruction, increased radiation background, and all, we're still better off today for fighting the totalitarians than we'd be if we'd knuckled under.''

"Borders could be changed at any time by mutual agreement," Quarles defended. "That's included in the concept of internal sovereignty. As for the rise of oppressive governments, well, I would like to give the world authority one more power: power to enforce a new and basic human right. Any person not charged with certain specific crimes—the usual ones, but political heresy and other forms of dissent are excluded—any person may leave his country.''

"And will any other country take him in?"

"I'm certain that many would, if he really was departing to escape tyranny. It would be a cheap way of undermining the tyrant. To be sure, a cynical caudillo could charge his opponents with murder and clap them in jail, but you can't do that very often if you're unpopular or you'll soon run out of jailers. It would become necessary to make oneself better liked.''

Quarles paused to sip from his glass. "You realize," he said, "I haven't any design for utopia. This is going to be a violent and not very happy world for a long time to come. That's why I wish that 'Egalitarianism' label could have been avoided. It suggests that there is a cure-all. But on the other hand, if such aims are to be worked for, there has to be some kind of organization to do the work, and I suppose it must inevitably have some kind of name. I do think we can take action to right the most outstanding wrongs and start ourselves, above all, back toward being free men."

The talk went on for several hours before Quarles bade them goodnight.

"Well?" said Gannoway eagerly, as soon as the door had closed.

"Good Lord," Koskinen gasped, "yes!"

XIV

THE Zodiac in Manhattan had seemed an odd place for the Egalitarian activist organization to keep local headquarters. It was fashionable and expensive enough to be patronized by numerous elite of MS, among others. But those men had assured themselves it was not bugged! And anyone might go to the place at any hour without attracting notice; and the use of masks was common; and in such a warren of curious rooms it would not be hard to maintain a meeting place.

Koskinen followed the others down through dimness and echoes. The shield unit felt heavy on his back. At the bottom a tunnel led to an armored door that opened after Gannoway had put his face in a hood to show the scanner his retinal patterns. The room beyond was large and austere, holding little but office equipment and a conference table.

Half a dozen men waited alertly. There was nothing in their appearance to suggest the typical 3D revolutionary. Their ages seemed to run from thirty to sixty, their clothes were conservative upper-middle class, and they went through the forms of introduction in a perfectly normal manner, Thomson, Washburn, Lanphier, Brorsen, Hill, Ricoletti. But Koskinen sensed the tension that thrummed in them. There was sweat on a couple of foreheads.

"I was able to get a quorum of this directing council on such short notice because each of us has an emergency cover, a plausible reason ready to advance for suddenly going off on a trip," Gannoway explained.

"We can't do it too often, though," Brorsen said sharply. "This better be for good cause tonight."

"It is. Suppose I turn the meeting over to our guests."

When he had finished, more than an hour later, and answered more excited questions than he wished to count, Koskinen was hoarse. He sat down and gulped the coffee offered him. Trembecki, who had said little, remained on his feet. One by one the council members ended their examination of the generator and went back to their own chairs. Cigarette smoke hazed the air.

Gannoway, at the head of the table, broke the silence. "The uses of this thing are obvious, especially after some further development work has been done," he said. "And I'll bet we find plenty more uses as we go along. Given material shielding against laser beams, even this little gadget is invulnerable to almost anything short of an atomic bomb; and a bigger one——! With that kind of equipment, you wouldn't need but a small army, some thousands of men, to take over the country."

"Wait a minute," Trembecki said. "Pete and I haven't yet agreed to anything. Especially not to a revolution."

"What had you in mind?" challenged Washburn.

Trembecki outlined Abrams's plans.

"Very pretty," Lanphier snorted. "Now tell me something that might work."

"Why shouldn't this?"

"To begin with, the risk scares me spitless. Supposing you have the President's full cooperation, and that's a big if by itself, do you believe Hugh Marcus will sit still for that kind of treatment? Even on a strictly legal plane—and we've no reason to believe he'll confine himself to that—he has his own lobby in Washington and his own propaganda machine. He can argue that the shield effect can't be kept secret forever, any more than the atomic bomb could be, if foreigners are allowed to do research on it. Therefore, he can say, MS needs more power than before, not less."

"He'd be arguing against public heroes, though," Trembecki said, "the men, notably Pete, who've presented this design to the United States."

"Huh! Heroes can get tarnished mighty quick."

"Not necessarily. Remember, legitimate charges can be brought against MS, of exceeding its authority and even attempting murder."

"To which it will be replied that Mr. Koskinen is a liar, or at least that he misunderstood the situation and panicked. That his shipmates were taken into custody to protect them from the Chinese—which is partly true, considering the fact that Captain Twain actually was murdered. That they were PI'd as an unavoidable measure, since in this emergency MS had to have total information fast.'' Lanphier shrugged. ''Oh, Marcus might have to sacrifice a few scrapegoats, agents he can say got too rough on their own initiative, without his knowledge. But he can keep his own skin whole, all right.''

''With the President gunning for him?''

''Yes, even then. You underestimate the hold that MS has on the public imagination. The American people have come to take it for granted that the Norris Doctrine is the only alternative to thermo-nuclear war. And the Norris Doctrine does logically require that there be an MS.''

''You see,'' Gannoway put in, ''no matter how well your scheme works out, it does not much alter the Protectorate. Does it, now?''

''Not overnight,'' Trembecki admitted. ''But under all circumstances, the United States will have exclusive possession of the shields for a number of years. Remember, an entire new concept of physics underlies the effect, based largely on extraterrestrial ideas that don't come easily to the human mind. It'll take quite a while for any foreign worker to duplicate, unaided by the Martians.

''So there will be a decade or better in which this country is not only supreme but safe. The fear will ease off. Reason will have a chance to operate again. You Egalitarians will be heard with respect.

I think I can promise that my boss will throw his influence behind your political campaigns. And that amounts to a lot more than his personal fortune. Quite a few powerful men have a high regard for Nathan Abrams's opinions."

"Considering what you've seen and done in your own life," Gannoway said, "I'm astonished at how high you rate human rationality."

Trembecki's laugh held scant humor. "I rate it lower than you, I suspect. But as for rationality *per se*, yes, I do have a high opinion of it, and I believe it should be encouraged whenever there's a chance. This is such a chance. No more than that; events could go completely awry; but who was ever guaranteed anything in this life?"

The councillors looked at each other. Finally Gannoway lit a fresh cigarette, drew deeply on it, and trickled smoke between his lips as he answered:

"You're right, any course of action is hazardous. The problem is how to minimize the hazard. As you ought to know, Jan, one way is to reduce the number of unknowns you have to deal with. Now I have a pretty fair understanding of myself and of my friends here, and you two fellows, and Nat. But I've never met the President, and you're no intimate of his yourself. Nor have we met the thousands of Congressmen, bureaucrats, military officers, business and labor officials, and so on, who constitute the power structure in this country. We certainly have not met every one of a quarter billion Americans, whose hopes and fears and hates and loves and beliefs and prejudices form the general environment within which the power structure must operate. Put so many unknowns together, let them interact freely, and we can't possibly predict what will happen. Yet that's what you propose to do—merely hoping for the best!''

Trembecki gave him a squint-eyed stare. ''You're arguing that force is the only predictable factor,'' he said.

''Yes,'' Gannoway replied. ''Isn't it? If I asked a stranger to do something for me, he might or might not. But if I pulled a gun on him, I'd know damn well he would.''

''Mm, I could name you some exceptions. But let that go. Precisely how do you want us to act?''

''I can't give you any details. We've had no time to think them out. But I do say we should keep the shield in our own hands, where we can know how it's going to be used. Proceed with development work and production of improved models——''

''Wait a minute,'' Koskinen objected. ''That'll take a long time. What about my shipmates?''

''There's that,'' Gannoway agreed. ''Also, Nat won't stand for his boy being kept locked away indefinitely, and he'll have to be persuaded not to contact the President. . . . Okay. Given a few shields of the present model—they could be turned out rather fast, couldn't they?—we can spring our friends. Including some Equals now in MS jails, too.''

''Get them out by actual attack?'' Washburn asked. He doubled a fist. ''Sure, I see how. A shield unit protecting a small, armed flitter, or something like that. First we nab some MS men and PI out of them where the prisoners are being held. Then we hit.''

"When we have our improved shields," Gannoway said, "we proceed to the next phase: the neutralization of MS."

"By shooting up its agents and establishments?" Trembecki said.

"Sometimes. More often, though, we'd simply stand them off while we carried out other operations."

"MS is an agency of the United States government. You're preaching insurrection."

"All right, I am."

"What do you expect other agencies will do meanwhile? Will the Army stay passive? Will Congress or the President make approving noises?"

"No."

"Or the people, even?"

"We'll be waging an intensive propaganda campaign, of course."

"Insufficient, when you're bearing arms against the United States. The Constitution defines that as treason."

"George Washington was called a traitor too, in his revolution."

"I'm not using loaded words. I'm just pointing out that when you've said A you have got to say B." Trembecki's forefinger stabbed at the men around the table. "Come on, admit it. Your aim is and always has been the violent overthrow of the United States government."

"So be it," Ricoletti said fiercely. "There's no other way."

"That means that a paramilitary junta will seize power and rule by fiat. It also means that the lid will be taken off the world. What do you expect will happen then?''

''Nothing very alarming,'' Gannoway said. ''This is one problem we have studied in detail. We aren't bearded anarchists huddling in some dank cellar, Jan. We know as much about war games, strategic analysis, and political anthropology as they do at West Point. And we've used such techniques for years to help us plan.

''The military garrisons abroad won't be recalled. Even with MS gone, they'll be able to keep control for quite some time. A large-scale revolt can't be organized and equipped overnight, you know. Meanwhile the Equal regime will be acting—fast. That is one very real advantage a junta has over a republican government or a bureaucracy, provided it knows what it wants: speed and decisiveness. As soon as internal order has been restored, we'll call an international conference. We already know who most of the delegates will be. We'll present them with Quarles's world authority scheme, get that ratified, staff the necessary organizations—then bring home the American troops, resign our own powers, and sit back to enjoy a world we've made fit to live in!''

XV

IT was very late, approaching sunrise, when Koskinen and Trembecki returned to their suite. But neither felt able to sleep.

Koskinen put the generator down on the floor, seated himself, jumped up again, got a drink of water, stared out the window at the darkling city, ground a fist into his palm and swore. Trembecki lit a cigar. His broad face had gone altogether hard.

"What should we do, Jan?" Koskinen asked finally.

"Get out of here," Trembecki said at once. "I'm not sure where to, though. By now MS probably has every one of Nat's places staked out."

Koskinen turned around to see him. "Do you mean that? About our leaving?"

"Uh-huh. If we stay here, we have to go along with the Equals. I see no way of talking them into a moderate course."

"They . . . they could be right, you know."

Trembecki grunted.

"I mean, well, they're so obviously sincere," Koskinen said.

"Most overrated virtue in the universe, sincerity."

"I don't know. I mean . . . look, when I signed on the *Boas* I took an oath to support the Constitution. It may sound schoolboyish, but I still take that oath pretty seriously. Now the Equals are asking me to violate it."

"So they are."

"But at the same time—there have been justified revolutions in the past."

"I doubt that."

"How about our own?"

"That was a different breed of cat. Remember, it started as an attempt merely to get certain traditional rights the colonists were entitled to as Englishmen. It became a national breakaway because this really was a nation, at least in embryo. The colonists had already ceased to be Englishmen. A revolt against foreign oppression is easy to justify. But an internal revolution, no."

"Even against domestic oppression? How about the French Revolution?"

"You should go back and re-read your history texts. The French Revolution proper did not deliberately employ violence. It didn't even abolish the monarchy. It simply used political pressure to bring about a number of long overdue reforms. But then the extremists, of right and left, got the bit between their teeth, and that's what led to the Reign of Terror and Napoleon. The original Russian Revolution was quite analogous. The Duma made the Czar abdicate, again by perfectly legal means. The Bolsheviks overthrew by force a functioning republic. I could give you a good many other examples.''

''There must be cases, though——''

''Yes, some. Various people have shot their way out from under a tyrant, now and then. But by definition, almost, they became the next despots, possibly benevolent, but still despots. And benevolent despotism is *not* the best form of government. It's stultifying.

''Once in a very great while, such a dictator has worked to bring freedom, by patiently overhauling the social structure. Kemal Atatürk is the most famous of the few who did. Now that's what you might call a righteous revolutionary. But you'll note he did his job slowly and carefully, and without holding a gun at people's heads.''

''Skip your ancient history,'' Koskinen snapped. ''We're here and now. Why shouldn't the Equals be like Atatürk? Is there any other way than theirs to get a world federation?''

''There might well be, assuming that it really is desirable, a matter which you haven't taken the time to probe very deeply. Myself, I doubt that establishing it by orders from above, the way Gannoway proposes, would work. There'd be too few people used to thinking in such terms to man its organizations. Things like that can't be built in a day, they have to grow.''

''When will the chance to grow be given? Honestly, Jan, I'm not fueled about a Glorious Vision of the Future or any such nonsense. I'm trying with everything I've got to decide what's right. I don't see how you can argue with what

Quarles said, that the unavoidable necessities of Pax Americana really are eroding away the spirit of the Constitution, making a dead letter of it. Isn't a radical breakthrough to different conditions the only chance of preserving what it stands for?''

Trembecki's cigar end glowed and dulled, glowed and dulled. ''That may be true,'' he said. ''Probably is, in fact. But there are many sorts of radicalism. The kind which would force itself on people, whether they want it or not, is the kind that I want no part of. Nor do you, if you'll stop to think about it.

''Look, Pete, what they glossed over down in that room was the fact that we have not yet exhausted our peaceful resources. Our backs are not quite to the wall. Marcus is not the omnipresent demon they make him out to be, nor is the President the feeble bungler which is the best they're willing to admit he might be. They talked about public support for MS and completely ignored the public opposition which also exists—as witness the above-board part of the Egalitarian movement, among many other things. They're fanatics, and that type has always ignored—been congenitally unable to see—any facts that won't fit their own preconceptions. That's Marcus's trouble too, you know. He's not so much hungry for personal power, though of course that element does operate in him, as he is saddled by a religious conviction that foreigners are evil and he alone knows how to save civilization. Do you want to trade one Marcus for another?''

''But Gannoway said,'' Koskinen stumbled,

"he said the junta would resign as soon as—"

"The world has heard that song before, my boy. If the Equals ever did seize the wheel, their dictatorship would be no more 'transitional' than that of any other revolutionary group. They'd have to stay on top for a while, simply to assure themselves their world arrangement was working out okay. And of course it wouldn't—new institutions always go off on unforeseen tangents—so they'd shoot some people and tinker with the machinery and wait again. Meanwhile it'd be necessary to proceed against those of their fellow citizens who couldn't stomach dictatorship. This implies a secret police a good deal stronger than MS is right now. And such an organization soon becomes a power in its own right; look at the history of every repressive government for proof. No, when you try to force the whole world, beginning with your own country, into the rigid framework of an ideology, you have to be an utterly ruthless tyrant. There's no other way."

"Quarles wouldn't let them!"

"What'd he have to say about it? He's only a well-meaning theorist. If he saw the truth and protested to Gannoway, they'd simply play the Grand Inquisitor scene over again.

"I don't know why I'm talking so abstractly, though," Trembecki finished. "You need only ask yourself how far anybody can be trusted who's willing to achieve his ends by the means Gannoway spelled out to us."

Stillness fell on the room. Koskinen sat down and stared at his generator. *Why did I bring it back?* he wondered. *Why was I born?*

A noise recalled him to awareness. Vivienne's bedroom door had slid open. She came out in nightgown and robe. The light gleamed on her tousled hair.

"I thought I heard you talking," she said.

"When'd you get in?" Trembecki asked.

"Around midnight. I couldn't take any more. Besides, I'd learned as much as I probably would be able to."

"Like what?"

She took a cigarette from a box on the table and lit it before saying tonelessly: "I played the part of a gang boss, or rather the female partner of a gang boss, come here for some gambling and so forth —and, on the side, to make discreet inquiries about possible business deals. A very natural thing; every place like this has underworld connections, and with Zigger gone, others will want to take over his territories. I got companionable with one or two of the girls who have been here long enough to know quite a bit. And frankly, I flirted with the night manager, with an implication that we might get still friendlier if he obliged me. What it boils down to is that I found out who really owns the Zodiac."

"Well?"

"An unregistered corporation of which the major stockholder, under a different name, is one Carson Gannoway."

"*What?*" Koskinen leaped to his feet.

Trembecki was not surprised. "I rather thought so," he said. "This place is laid out and operated so very conveniently for the Equals. Obviously, they don't want it so much for a headquarters as a source of funds. Financing is the big problem of every revolutionary organization."

"Oh, no, no, no," Koskinen shuddered.

Decision sprang up in him, tight and cold. "We're leaving," he said. "Get dressed, Vee."

"Are you that shocked?" she asked.

"No, this only clinches the matter for him," Trembecki said. "Go on, make yourself ready. I'll explain meanwhile."

He did so, curtly. Koskinen paced the floor, back and forth, his palms and armpits chill with sweat. Where to go? What to do? Was it possible to get back to Abrams's home? Trembecki believed not, and he should know. Besides, to compromise Leah was unthinkable.

Wait . . . hadn't Vee once mentioned an upstate hideaway of Zigger's? Yes, he remembered now. It should serve for a while, at least, give a breathing spell in which they could think of something better. He told Trembecki about it, and the Pole agreed: "We can probably get a cab yet, even if the alarm is out. If we take a zigzag route, changing pretty often, I'd say we have a fair chance of making it. Are you ready, Vee?"

"Right now." She emerged from her room in the dress she had worn here, purse clipped to the belt. "Think it'd help to wear masks?"

"Only till we're out of the building. Then they're too conspicuous. Where'd I put mine?"

The main door opened. Trembecki whirled, snatching for his gun. He wasn't fast enough. "Stop where you are!" Gannoway barked. His own pistol covered them. The other councillors, likewise armed, crowded behind him.

"You didn't think we wouldn't put a tap on this place and hear your opinions of us, did you?" Gannoway said.

XVI

"PETE! The generator!" Vivienne cried.

It was on Koskinen's back. He spun the adjustment wildly, hoping to expand the field so it would include her and Trembecki, and threw the switch as Hill's gun spat.

Too little, too late. Silence thundered at him. The bullet fell harmless to the floor. Ricoletti charged and rebounded, six feet from Koskinen. But Brorsen and Lanphier had seized Vivienne by the arms. Thomson and Washburn did the same to Trembecki. Gannoway plucked the Pole's gun from its shoulder holster, tossed it on the sofa, and shut the door. The happenings were for Koskinen like a nightmare dumb show.

There was noise, before he closed us off, he thought. *Whoever heard—— No. What would be done here about a scream?*

Gannoway spoke to Vivienne. She answered him haughtily. The councillors argued among themselves. Gannoway shushed them with an imperious gesture, walked to the screen edge and looked at Koskinen for some time. Koskinen could only snarl at him.

Gannoway snapped his fingers. Opening a drawer, he took out a couple of minicoms. He scribbled on a piece of paper and held it where Koskinen could see.

"This is too clumsy a way of communication. I will toss one of these at you. If you switch your field off very briefly you can get it. I'll lay my gun down across the room so I can't reach it in that short a time. Those who aren't holding your partners will keep their hands in the air. Okay?"

Koskinen nodded. He wanted to shout something to Vivienne in the split second when the screen field wasn't between them, but he was too busy with his timing.

Insulated again, he put the instrument on his wrist. Gannoway turned the other one high, so it could detect anything spoken in the room, and laid it on a table. "Now we can talk," he said.

"There's nothing to talk about," Koskinen answered.

"On the contrary, there's everything. You've gotten a fantastically wrong idea about us."

"Everything you do makes it look more and more right."

"You were willing to listen to us in the conference room. Then Jan Trembecki poisoned your mind."

"He only showed me what the things really meant that you'd been advocating. I am not going to be a party to the murder of my fellow citizens."

"Go ahead and make an exception for some of them," Trembecki said.

Ricoletti stuck him in the face. "Hey, none of that," Gannoway ordered.

"What's a little roughness to a revolutionary?" Vivienne gibed.

"We want to be friends," Gannoway said.

"You can start by letting us go where we want to go."

"That's lunacy. You wouldn't last a week in the open. I can't permit something like the shield to fall to Marcus."

"Then help it fall to the President."

"I've explained to you——"

"We don't accept that explanation," Koskinen interrupted. "I'm supposed to turn this thing over to the proper authorities. You're not one of them."

"It's no use, Carse," Thomson growled. "They're fanatics."

"I'm afraid Jan is," Gannoway sighed. "But Pete, you seem like a reasonable man. Can't you see our point of view?"

"Yes," Koskinen said. "That's exactly the trouble."

"I hate to get tough. But you are immobilized in there. A man dies of thirst in a few days."

Koskinen was faintly astonished at his own lack of fear. He wanted to live as much as the next human being, or perhaps a little more so. But there didn't seem to be room in him for anything except anger. "I'm quite prepared for that," he retorted. "But then my body will be inside the screen forever, unless you wreck the generator with a heat ray. That won't help you to build another."

"Eventually we might."

"Not for a devil of a long time. Meanwhile, other men can go to Mars—Abrams could finance an expedition by himself if need be—whom the Martians would be willing to give the plans to."

"Yes. There is that, isn't there?" Gannoway brooded a moment.

When he looked up again, something terrible lay in his eyes. "You may not be afraid to die," he said, "but can you let your friends die, simply because of your own stubbornness?"

Trembecki spat on the floor. "Isn't he the big bad villain, though?"

"I mean it," Gannoway said. "I really do. It's that important."

Heat and cold pursued each other through Koskinen. "You kill them and you'll kill the last atom of a chance you ever had!" he yelled.

"I didn't mean immediate death," Gannoway said. "You could last three or four days in there. Given stimulants to help her along, Mrs. Cordeiro should be about equally durable."

The color drained out of Vivienne's face. She had to try twice before she could say, "Don't pay any attention to him, Pete. Whatever happens."

"You know where the equipment is," Gannoway told Hill and Ricoletti. "Bring it here."

The councillors went out. Ricoletti was grinning. Gannoway sat down and helped himself to a cigarette. "Go ahead and talk to each other," he invited mildly.

"Vee," Koskinen croaked.

She drew some long breaths before a degree of steadiness came. "Don't feel sorry for me, Pete.

I'm not interested in living, if the price is to help out creatures like these.''

"Wait a minute, you," Thomson protested. "You don't think we enjoy hurting anyone, do you?"

"Why, yes," Trembecki said. The councillors glared at him.

"I honor your motives," Gannoway said with a note almost of desperation. "You can't imagine how I'd like to have you as my friends. And you could contribute so much to the world. Do I look like a fiend? If this happens, will I ever get the blood off my hands?" his mouth twisted. "Only if I let you go, how much more blood will be shed?"

"Dry up," Trembecki said. To Koskinen: "I'm getting off easy, it seems. There's no percentage in their doing more than shooting me. But——" He blinked his eyes. Tears stood in them. "If I break first and tell you to turn off that field, Pete, don't listen to me, you hear?"

Koskinen paid him small heed. The terror had come upon him now, high and shouting. He saw Vivienne as if through a haze. "You decide," he begged her. "You're the only one who's got any right to."

"I've already decided," she said. "You stay put."

"No, listen, I mean it. What's all this politicking to you? If anything, you should want nothing more than revenge on Marcus. The Equals can promise you that, better than anybody else. This isn't your cause, Vee. I . . . we want you to be brave enough to choose for yourself."

She smiled ever so faintly. "You're being a

coward, Pete. You want to shift the responsibility."

"It's not one I can take," he wept.

"Okay, then, I'll take it. Stay put, Pete. My life hasn't been worth such a lot to me, these last several years. There's no great loss involved."

"Don't talk that way!"

"Hush, dear." She murmured to him, meaningless comfort, while Gannoway chain smoked. The councillors holding her and Trembecki shifted about in their unease. Time crawled.

"How about the you-know-what?" asked Trembecki suddenly.

The detonator! Koskinen remembered. A lunatic hope swerved through him. "Sure, I'll come out," he said. "Just release her . . . them . . . and I'll surrender."

"Come out first," Gannoway replied. "I'm not chancing any tricks."

"It's no good, Pete," Vivienne said. "An intact unit, that's too big a gift to give them."

"But if you get the chance, while I'm still inside the screen——" he whispered.

He wondered why she seemed so appalled at the thought of blowing his head off. It was better to die thus than from thirst and hunger, after watching her in pain. "No," she said shakily. "I can't. Not possibly."

"What's going on here, anyway?" Brorsen demanded.

Attention was diverted by the return of Hill and Ricoletti. They carried a heavy box with a handle and a large roll of plastic sheeting. "Where should we put this?" Hill asked.

Gannoway gulped, but decided: "Right there in that doorway to the bedroom. The force field is taking up too much space here in the parlor."

Ricoletti spread the sheet as directed. "Don't want to mess the rug," he chortled. Hill opened the box and tossed a coil of rope at Washburn's feet. "Tie that guy up," he suggested.

Trembecki drew a quick breath and whispered something in Polish. He made no resistance as he was led to a chair and lashed in place, but he called, "Pete." The third time Koskinen heard him.

"Yes, yes?"

"Pete. Look at me." Trembecki caught Koskinen's eyes and would not let go. "Listen. I'm a dead man. Whatever happens, short of the U.S. Marines bursting in the door, I've reached the end."

"No, no," Gannoway said. "Give me the shield and I hope you'll live many more years."

Trembecki ignored him. "Listen very carefully, Pete. *I don't mind*. I've enjoyed life, but I got over being scared of death a long time ago. I saw so much of it. And I've no dependents, my wife is dead, my children are grown. I can't think of a better way to go out than, well, helping freedom along a little . . . or a worse way to survive than being a slave. Do you understand?"

Koskinen nodded dumbly. He felt, through his heartbeat and dizziness, that Trembecki was trying to tell him something. But he could not think clearly enough to see what it was.

"If something should happen, if you get a chance, forget about me," Trembecki said. "I've had a full share of life. Vee is still young. So are you. And you're also the man with the shield to give the world.

"Once, back in Europe, I ordered a town shelled where some of my own men were kept prisoner. They died. But we had to reduce that town. I've never felt bad about it. You shouldn't either."

Gannoway rose, suspicious. "What's going on here? Shut up, Jan."

"Okay," Trembecki said. "Goodbye."

"Not yet," Gannoway said. He approached Koskinen. "Pete, do you realize what this means? She won't be herself very long. Toward the end, she won't even be human."

"So you've done it before," Vivienne said.

Gannoway bit his lip in exasperation. "We'll begin with a nerve machine," he said. "That doesn't do serious harm, if it isn't left on too long. Any time you want us to stop, we will. But if you don't——well——" He waved a hand at the instruments which Ricoletti was taking out of the box and laying on the floor.

Hill put a chair on the plastisheet in the bedroom doorway. Ricoletti plugged in the neural exciter. Brorsen and Lanphier led Vivienne to the chair and bound her fast.

"All right, stand back there," Gannoway said thickly. Ricoletti alone remained with Vivienne. The rest moved into the parlor again. Koskinen couldn't see Trembecki, who sat by the wall behind him. His vision was blurred anyway.

"Well, Pete?" Gannoway asked.

"No," Vivienne said. "See them in hell first."

Ricoletti began to clip the leads to her arms and legs.

"Pete!" Trembecki roared. *"Expand the field!"*

It was as if another body moved. Koskinen's hand flew to the adjustment knob. He twirled it toward maximum. Driven by the energy stored in the power pack, the force shell exploded outward. Only then did he comprehend what he had done.

He saw Gannoway smeared across the wall like an insect. And the rest of the council—— No, one man was jammed into a corner. The field swelled further, crushed him to red ruin. The walls cracked open. Shards fell from the ceiling. The window shattered outward and a table crashed through to the street.

Vivienne and Ricoletti were merely pushed into the bedroom. Koskinen snapped off the field and plunged toward them. Ricoletti lurched back out into the demolished parlor. He fumbled in a stunned fashion beneath his tunic. A gun came forth. Koskinen snatched a blade from the debris on the floor and charged him. The gun spat. A slug puffed dust an inch from Koskinen's feet. Then he was upon Ricoletti. He struck. The knife laid open the man's throat.

Ricoletti went down in blood and wreckage. Koskinen leaped over him, into the bedroom. "Vee!" he yelled. "Are you hurt?"

"No," she gasped. "Cut me loose, though. We've got to get out of here. This'll draw everybody in the house."

He hacked at the ropes. When he had finished, he threw the knife skittering across the floor. She got to her feet with more self-possession than he had. "Come on." She stopped only to pick a gun from the rubble and slip it into her purse. The main door, burst open, showed a hallway full of swirling dust.

Koskinen didn't look at the place where Trembecki had been. But he raised one hand as he went by.

A girl stood screaming in the corridor. Vivienne led Koskinen in the opposite direction. A male attendant ran around the corner of a side passage. "What happened?" he bawled.

"Something exploded, I think," Vivienne said. "We're going after help."

Her hand hovered near the purse, ready to draw and fire. But the man ran witlessly on. Vivienne took the hall down which he had come. The nearest upramp was crowded with excited humanity, but the escapees had the downramp to themselves and were not noticed. Two floors below, Vivienne took a corridor again. When they were out of sight around a corner, in a deserted stretch lined only with doors, she stopped to get her breath.

"We're clear," Koskinen said stupidly. "We're clear. We got away."

She leaned her arm against the wall and buried her face in the crook of it. "Jan didn't," she said through tears.

Koskinen took her about the waist. It was hard to say which gained more from the few minutes they held to each other.

In the end she raised her head and said with some life in her voice: "We'd better get out of here before they connect us with what's happened and start looking for us. And we've got to get out of town, too. Let me think. . . . Our suite was on the south side. Let's leave by the north entrance then, where the commotion won't have been noticed in the street. Get the generator off your back, Pete, and carry it in your hand. Less noticeable that way.''

They walked on at a normal pace. She took out comb and compact and made some repairs to her appearance as they went. ''What a man Jan was,'' she said once.

What a woman you are, he thought.

It seemed odd to him how neutral his emotions were with respect to those he had killed. Trembecki he mourned, of course, with the Pole's own absolution to preserve him from any sense of guilt. But as for the others, his enemies, he felt neither glad nor sorry. Their deaths were merely something that had happened, impersonal, already fading in his memory under the urgencies of escape.

XVII

THERE was morning in the sky when Koskinen and Vivienne stepped forth. Stars lingered to the west, but eastern spires were outlined against a climbing brilliance. The avenue lay still, an occasional groundcar sliding between great walls. The air felt unutterably cool and fresh.

"I suppose we are heading for Zigger's place," Koskinen said.

"Nowhere else to go, is there?" Vivienne responded.

"And then we'll try to get in touch with Abrams?"

"We can *try*," she said skeptically, "but if his lines aren't tapped by now, I miss my guess.

"And you know," she added, "there was some truth to the arguments those Equal people presented, at least as Jan reported them to me. Giving this thing to the Protectorate and expecting any real improvement is like asking a drug addict to cure himself with aspirin."

"Who else should we give it to?" he asked wearily.

"I don't know . . . I don't know. There's a taxi."

The driver pushed the door button for them and they got in. "Syracuse," Vivienne said. "I'll give you the exact address when we get there." That would be only the first of their stops, as they changed from car to car. The driver punched his controls, and Koskinen saw again a sunrise over the waters.

The blankout panel began to close off the front of the cab. "No," Vivienne said. "Stop. Retract that thing."

The driver looked surprised, but obeyed. "I . . . I like to watch the view in front, too," she said lamely. Since that was nothing but a sky, turning from silver to blue as the sun mounted, Koskinen doubted the driver was convinced.

Wait! She had leaned forward to give her order. Recollection struck into Koskinen. He reached around her back and snapped open her purse. "What the devil?" she exclaimed, and tried to twist about. His right hand stopped her with a grip on the arm. He pulled the detonator out and let her go. She crouched away from him, half angry and half afraid. "What's got into you, Pete?"

"I'm sorry, Vee," he said. "Please don't have any hard feelings. But the situation's changed again. From now on I want to make my own decisions." He dropped the case in a pocket of his blouse and sealed the flap.

"You could have asked me for it."

"Yes, and you might have said no. After all,

you refused to use it once already. I'm grateful to you for that. But I've been too passive. It's high time I became my own boss."

She let out a long breath. Muscle by muscle she relaxed. The smile she gave him was slow and warm. "You're toughening fast, I see," she murmured.

He flushed. "Have to, I suppose." With returning unease he noticed how the driver watched them in his rearview. Why hadn't Vee wanted the privacy panel shut?

The call screen told Koskinen why, two minutes later. "Attention all vehicles! Attention all vehicles! This is an hourly announcement from the Bureau of Military Security. Two criminals are at large, foreign agents whose arrest is of the utmost importance. They may be riding in a public——"

Vivienne's gun was already out of her purse and aimed at the driver's head. "Not a move, asco," she ordered. "Don't let your hands go anywhere near that transmission switch."

"——considered extremely dangerous," the crisp voice said. In the screen Koskinen saw his own face, from the tape that had been made during his second call, and a photograph of Vivienne that had been gotten somewhere. "If you see these persons, you are required by the National Defense Act to——"

"I thought you looked . . . sorta familiar," the driver stammered. "What's going on? What do you want?"

"You won't get hurt if you cooperate," Vivienne said.

"Look, I got a wife and kids. I——please——"

Koskinen glanced out the window and down. At this speed, the densest part of town had been left behind. The land was still dominated by roofs, but they belonged to relatively small buildings and traffic was light.

"You can't get nowhere in this car," the driver said frantically. "Not in any car. If they really suspect you're in a car, Control'll take everything past the police checkpoints."

"That's rather extreme," Koskinen said. "I should think it'd tie up traffic from now till midnight. They haven't done it yet, have they?"

Vivienne threw him a haggard glance. "They haven't exhausted all their other leads yet, either," she said. "Sooner or later, though, they'll try a mass car check. If they get word of what just happened at the Zodiac—and they will; there're MS customers in the place—they'll pretty quickly deduce what's happened. And then their logical move will be to try and trap us in our escape vehicle. The driver's right. We'd better get out of this hack while we can."

"But——I mean, how——"

"I don't know, I don't know. . . . Wait. Yes. Stop at that playground yonder."

They slanted down, went off Control, touched an old and cracked street, and halted at the curb. The playground stretched vacant and the houses opposite—peak-roofed, narrow-windowed, with peeling stucco fronts, obviously prewar survivals—hardly showed more life at this hour. Vivienne opaqued the windows and suggested Koskinen bind and gag the driver.

"I'll use my own clothes for that," Koskinen

said, "and wear his. Somebody may remember what I had on at the Zodiac."

"Good idea. You are becoming a fine outlaw." She waited while he swapped garments. Afterward he found some cord in the tool compartment, with which he did a thorough job of securing the prisoner on the rear floor.

"Somebody will get curious and investigate, sometime today," he assured the man. "You'll excuse me for hoping it won't be for a few hours."

"Oh, oh," said Vivienne, standing beside the taxi. "Man coming."

Koskinen emerged and locked the doors. A burly person in mechanic's coveralls halted his slouching walk and said, "Trouble, bud? Maybe I can help."

"Thanks," Koskinen said, "but the company wants me to report direct in case of breakdowns. Also, my fare has to get on her way. Where's the nearest tube?"

The mechanic regarded him sharply. "No tubes this far out."

"Oh." Koskinen laughed. "I'm fresh from Los Angeles. Still feeling my way around. Where's a monorail station?"

"I'm headed there myself."

Koskinen was pleased at how readily he answered questions about the west coast, where he had never been either. It took the mechanic's mind off the generator, which he probably assumed belonged to the lady. The man couldn't afford to travel, with wages as low as they were, "thanks to them machines. I'm lucky to have a job at all. If that there Antarctic colony had only worked out the way they talked about, I'd've gone like a shot. Chance to be my own boss."

"Expensive, though, isn't it?"

"Yeah. That's the catch. Need shelter against the cold. That costs money. So only the big companies or the government can build. So nobody can go who's not on their payroll. And everybody has to live cheek by jowl because one big shelter costs less than a lotta little ones. Right? I decided I might as well stay here, the way the colony worked out in practice."

Too bad, Koskinen thought. *Americans were free men once.*

Luckily there were no taxis waiting at the station—if this poor decayed suburb rated any such service. Koskinen entered a phone booth and pretended to call one for Vivienne. The mechanic boarded the train which had just come in. As it started again, Vivienne led Koskinen in a run and mounted a car further down.

"This is aimed our way, all right," she panted, "but we don't want our friend to know that. It's a small miracle that he didn't recognize us from the bulletins. The next time he sees one, he probably will remember."

Koskinen nodded. They took a seat. There were only a few sleepy, drably-clad fellow passengers, and he doubted if the coach was ever filled. Employment had dropped far below transportation capacity.

You know, he thought, *people like this aren't really restricted to three choices, crime, the dole, or a dull and meaningless job. With modern power tools as cheap as they are, with small machines as well, with biological fuel cells to furnish low-cost energy, with the food-growing techniques developed for extraterrestrial bases—a family could become self-sufficient. Home industries could revive, not so much competing with the big automatic factories as ignoring them. And that trend would eventually force the economy as a whole to use automation rationally.*

The brief excitement died in him. *I can't be the first to daydream along those lines. I can already see why nothing like it has been tried. Big business, big labor, big government wouldn't sit still for such a development. They'd clamp down with zoning laws, regulations, taxes, anything that came to hand, because a nation of independent men would spell the end of their power. . . . My! I seem to've gotten cynical at the same astounding rate Vee thinks I've gotten tough. But I can't help it, I can* sense *the wrongness in society today, as clearly as I can sense it in a badly designed engine.*

That reminded him. "How are we going to get to our destination?" he asked Vivienne. "Control can stop anything we'd likely be able to hire or steal."

"Yes. Except——" She stared out the window. The suburb was giving way to open fields, where dew flashed in the young sunlight.

"I've gotten an idea," she said. "The World War One Centennial Commission has built a lot of replica machines. They're for reenacting battles as the appropriate dates roll around. Makes a nice 3D spectacle, and gives idle people something to play with—but the planes and guns and ground-cars are honest working reproductions. Between assignments they're occasionally used in advertising stunts, or as a demonstration for history classes, or what have you. Well, a batch of the airplanes is kept right in this area.''

"Huh?"

"They haven't any autopilots. So they can flit about freely. That's no traffic hazard. As slow as they are, anybody's radar can spot them in ample time to dodge, and Control routinely compensates for bigger swerves than that. What matters to us is that the police can't take over a vehicle from a distance if it doesn't have an autopilot. Also, no one except the persons immediately concerned pays much attention to where those planes go. They don't file flight plans or any such thing.''

"My God." Koskinen pulled his jaw back into place.

"Zigger and I visited out there one day last year. I know the layout. If you can figure out some way to steal one, the theft won't be noticed for days. I could be wrong, of course. What do you say?''

He realized that she had made a final surrender of leadership to him. It was a heavy burden. He swallowed and said, "Sure. We'll try.''

XVIII

THE planes were stored three miles from the nearest train stop. Koskinen and Vivienne walked there, after buying breakfast and two lengths of rope at the supermarket, as well as some pills to compensate for sleeplessness. Most of the way they followed a narrow, crumbling street lined with the mean houses of a moribund village. Trucks, occasional cars, go-carts with bubble canopies whirred past them. But there were only a few other pedestrians—chiefly women, though some unemployed and sullen men—and nobody paid the strangers much attention. One man indicated where to turn, baffled that anyone went to the hanger on foot but too apathetic to ask why. Evidently, Koskinen thought, the general indifference to life these days was working against Marcus's bulletins about him. Nobody bothered to be alert, or even to notice what the strangers looked like.

The side street petered out in a lane which crossed an enormous stretch of vacant lot.

"Ugh," said Vivienne. "Weeds and brambles where homes stood once, before the firestorm. It gives me the crawls."

"Eh?" Koskinen blinked at her. The grasses rippled silvery green. Somewhere a bird was singing. Instead of dust he smelled moist earth. "But this is lovely."

"Ah, well." She squeezed his arm. "I'm a city girl at heart."

"Why is the hangar way out here, anyway?"

"Land's cheap that nobody else wants."

The building and airstrip stood in the middle of the field, surrounded by a twelve-foot electrified fence. Radar alarms would alert the village police if anyone tried to land an unauthorized aircar here. So a watchman wasn't needed, and there was no activity scheduled for today. Koskinen looked around with care. None of the houses he saw were so close that he was likely to be noticed.

He made a noose in one rope and, after several tries, threw it around the top of a fencepost. "Okay, Vee," he said, and helped her don the shield generator. She turned it on. He used the second rope to lash himself to the outside of the potential barrier, and passed the lariat's end through a loop in that harness. Awkwardly, then, he shoved her against the fence and pulled them both up hand over hand, the invisible shell between him and the charged mesh. He sweated to think what would happen if he touched it. He might survive the shock, but not the aftermath of the alarms that were sure to go off.

At the top he hung on one-handed while he knotted lasso and harness together. Taking the lasso's end in his teeth, he untied himself and crawled over the shell of force until he could leap. He fell clear of the fence on the inside. The impact was jarring. When he had his breath back, he hauled on the lariat until Vivienne in her invisible cocoon tilted over the top of the wires. Then he swayed back and forth like a bellringer, until she bumped the fence and rebounded through a considerable arc. At the far end of one such swing, she cut off the screen field and fell clear of the harness that had bound it. Nevertheless, she landed so close to the fence that his heart stopped for a moment.

She picked herself up. "Okay, we're in." Actual laughter sounded beneath the wind. "Koskinen and Cordeiro, Cat Burglars by appointment to His Majesty Tybalt I, King of the Cats. C'mon, let's swipe us some transportation."

They crossed more weeds and the tarmac airstrip to the hangar. Vivienne would have shot out the lock if necessary, but the door opened for them as they neared. The space within was huge and dim. Koskinen gaped about at the machines. Somehow they made him feel he had wandered into a more ancient past than even the towers on Mars. *You see*, he told himself, *this is my past. My great-grandfather must have ridden in a car like these.*

This is my planet. Anger gathered in him. *I don't like what they have done to her.*

He suppressed emotion, got some tools off a workbench, and busied himself. In an hour he had chosen his vehicle. The nameplate called it a De Havilland 4 day bomber, a big two-winged machine, two open cockpits, less dash than the Spads or Fokkers but a certain unpretentious ruggedness that pleased him. Between an operator's manual and his Mars-taught feeling for rightness, he deduced how to fly it. They rolled it out onto the strip, fuelled it from a pump, and turned off the radar sentinels.

"Take the rear seat and use the auxiliary controls to start her," he told Vivienne. "I showed you how. I'll crank the propeller."

She regarded him with a sudden intensity. "We might crash, or get shot down, or anything, you know," she said.

"Yes." He shrugged. "That's been understood right along."

"I——" She took his hands. "I want you to know something. In case I don't get another chance to tell you."

He looked into the brown eyes and waited.

"That detonator," she said. "It's a fake."

"What?"

"Or I should say, the detonator works but the bomb doesn't." Her laugh caught in her throat. "When Zigger told me to make that thing for you . . . we'd been talking half the night, you and I, remember? . . . I couldn't do it. There's no explosive in that capsule. Only talcum powder."

"What?" he whispered again.

"I didn't tell them at Abrams's place. They'd have substituted a real bomb then, and I'd never have been able to trigger it but someone else might have. Now—— Well, I wanted you to know, Pete."

She tried to withdraw her hands, but he caught

them and wouldn't let go. "That's the truth, Vee?"

"Yes. Why should you doubt me?"

"I don't," he said. He rallied his entire courage, drew the detonator from his pocket, and snicked off the safety. She watched him through tears. He pressed the button.

With a whoop, he tossed the object into the weeds, kissed her with inexpert violence, stammered something about her being his crewmate and Sharer-of-Hopes and much else, kissed her again, and lifted her bodily to the rear cockpit. She nestled among the machine guns there and took the stick in a dazed fashion. He swung the heavy wooden propeller down with more strength than he had known he had.

The engine coughed to life. Exhaust fumes grew pungent in his nose. He sprang onto the lower wing and thence to the front seat. Vivienne relinquished her own controls. Koskinen spent a minute listening to the engines and noting the many vibrations. It seemed right to him. He taxied forward, accelerating. The plane left earth with a joyous little jump unlike anything he had ever felt before.

Vivienne had shown him their destination on a map. He found he could follow the landmarks without much trouble at this leisurely pace. Elkor's training of nerves and muscles made piloting simple after the first few minutes.

The plane was a roaring, shuddering, odorous, cranky thing to fly. But fun. He had never before been so intimate with the air. It howled around his windshield, lashed his face, thrummed in the struts, sang in the wires, and bucked against the control surfaces. Ridiculous, he thought, that he should draw so much life and hope from a primitive machine, or even from learning that the woman with him had never been willing to help with his murder. But that was the way he felt. And the landscape below had grown altogether fresh, open, fair; this was a wealthy district, where houses were big and far between, separated by woods and parklands. The Hudson gleamed between hills that were infinitely many hues of green, under a blue sky and scudding white clouds. There must be an answer to his dilemma—in such a world!

There was. He saw it with wonder. After a very long while he looked upward. *"Dream well, Elkor,"* he called.

XIX

AT the end of two days' hard work, it was good to stand for a while and become one with the land. Zigger's retreat overlooked the river, which ran like fire beneath the westering sun. Steep forested slopes rose from the opposite shore. On this side, the view off the terrace was of lawns and rosebeds that sloped down to the water. Oak leaves rustled above Koskinen, an apple tree stood heavy with fruit, a fir sighed in the breeze, a thrush chirped. The million scents bewitched him.

But "now" is an infinitesimal. As the pleasant weariness of labor began to leave his body, his mind took possession and he could no longer feel joy.

Why not? he asked himself. *My job's done, the shelter's finished. Our word is already out to the world. And we still have peace.*

We won't much longer . . .

We'll have it again, or be dead.

Can't say I want to be dead.

What happened next, and how soon, depended

on how fast his enemies could trace him. The airplane might well have been seen to land here. Certainly it had left a clear mark, plowing up the golf course with the rear skid that it used in lieu of wheel brakes. Nobody in the village, a few miles away, suspected that he and Vivienne had burgled their way into the house. The locals must be used to odd goings-on at Mr. Van Velt's place; and Vivienne was known to them, under a different name. It was unlikely, too, that she would be identified with the hunted woman. She had tricks of makeup and expression that made her look utterly different from the broadcast picture, without appearing a stranger to the deliverymen from the stores.

Nevertheless, there was bound to be gossip. Why was she here alone, without Mr. Van Velt or a servant or anything? Why had she ordered a midget bulldozer sent to the place, a fork lift truck, a mess of lumber and concrete blocks, when she arrived yesterday? Some official might hear the story and begin wondering himself.

From the other end of the trail, too, there were probably clues pointing in this direction. Men must have been captured by MS at the Crater, and some of them doubtless knew about this country estate, and interrogation might bring out what they knew. The enemy was efficient.

Doubts assailed Koskinen. His hopes were tenuous, after all, based on little more than a feeling of how cause and effect ought to develop in a rational world; and surely this world was anything but rational. Might it not be best to flee on?

No. Sooner or later, you had to make a stand. Koskinen drew another breath of Earth's air.

Vivienne emerged through the French doors. "Whew!" she said. "I'm hoarse as a frog and my fingertips are raw from button pushing. I do hope you'll agree I've called enough people, while you were making that fortress."

"I'm sure you have," he said. "We may as well relax now."

"Wonderful. I'll rustle up a real supper to celebrate."

"You mean heat *two* packages?" he teased.

"I do not. I mean an old-fashioned individually prepared supper, using my own hands and brain in the making. I really am a fair cook." The forced lightness left her tone. She came to stand beside him. "We won't have many more chances."

"Maybe not," he admitted. "Perhaps a few days, though."

She laid an arm about his waist and her head on his shoulder. "I wish I could do something more for you, Pete, than just make you a meal."

"Why?" His face turned hot. He stared fixedly across the river.

"I owe you so much."

"No. Nothing. You've saved me . . . I don't know how many times . . . and still it's little compared to that business of the locket." He touched the chain. "I don't think I ever want this taken off."

"Does it mean that much to you, Pete? Really?"

"Yes. Because you see . . . you suddenly became someone I belong with, the way I do with my shipmates. I can't ever repay you that."

"You know," she whispered, "that's pretty much the way I feel about you."

Abruptly she pulled free of him and ran back into the house. He wondered why, and wanted to follow her, but checked himself. The situation was delicate, the two of them alone here, and he didn't want to risk spoiling that which he saw developing by too great a haste.

However, his restlessness had been aroused. He felt a need to do something. *Might as well make a few more calls while she fixes that meal,* he decided. *The more the better*. He went into the living room and threaded his way among luxurious furniture to the phone.

The note pad showed him that Vivienne, on her last batch of messages, had covered half a dozen numbers in different cities of India. The Americas and Europe had previously been taken care of. Koskinen reflected upon his school geography. Where would be a strategic place to try next? The idea was to scatter the information as widely as possible.

China? No, he couldn't quite bring himself to that. The average Chinese was a decent, kindly man . . . of course . . . the average anybody was. But the current government of China—— Okay, let the Chinese find out from someone else. Koskinen punched for the operator. "English-language Tokyo directory," he said.

With a helpfully inhuman lack of curiosity, the robot flashed a page onto his screen. Koskinen turned the reel knob until he came to the listing for Engineers. He copied down several home and office numbers at random, cleared the board, and punched the first number, adding the RX which internationally directed the receiving instrument to record. A flat Oriental face looked out at him, puzzled. This job was easier when no one was at home.

"I am Peter Koskinen," he rattled. He had spelled Vivienne occasionally in the past couple of days. He offered a mechanical smile. "News service will confirm for you that I have lately returned from Mars with the *Franz Boas* expedition. I have brought with me a device which confers virtual invulnerability on the user. To prevent its suppression, I am publicizing the physical principles, engineering specifications, and operating instructions on a worldwide basis."

The Japanese got a word in edgewise, doubtless to the effect that he didn't speak English and this was some mistake. Koskinen held the first sheet of his treatise up to him, then the next and the next, as fast as he was able. (Preparing it hadn't been a very long job, since he and Vivienne recalled quite clearly the plans they had drawn in the Crater.) A few people had switched off, impatient with an obvious lunatic, but this man watched with growing interest. Koskinen felt sure he'd take his tape to someone who could read a playback, frame by frame. And if only a fraction of the many who had been called would try the gadget out, word would get around—inevitably.

Koskinen finished, said goodbye, and started on the next number. Vivienne's shout interrupted him.

He cursed and dashed back onto the terrace.

She poised there, bowstring taut, pointing into the sky. Four long black aircars whistled down the evening sunbeams. He saw the Military Security emblem on their flanks.

"I spotted them from the kitchen window." Vivienne's voice wavered. "So soon?"

"We must have left a clearer trail for them than I hoped."

"But——" She caught his hand in cold fingers and struggled not to cry.

"Come on," he urged. They returned to the living room, picked up the screen generator, and hurried out onto the patio in the rear. It was a wide flagstoned area surrounded by willows and roses, the clear view making it a good place for a stand. Koskinen had torn up much of the floor with the 'dozer, dug a pit and roofed it with concrete blocks. Food packages, miscellaneous containers of water, bedding, and such necessities were stowed within. There was also a rifle from Zigger's gun cabinet, and a minicom for parley purposes. Koskinen took the shield generator down inside and flipped the switch.

He had adjusted it so the barrier shell enclosed the little blockhouse and a section of outside floor in a cylindroid about twenty feet long. The flagstones made a loud crack as the field, expanding from zero to finite thickness, cut them in two. Then stillness descended.

"Okay," Koskinen said. "We're safe now, Vee-vee."

She crept into his arms, buried her face against his breast and trembled.

"What's wrong?" He laid his other hand below

her chin and tilted her face toward his. "Aren't you glad we can start hitting back?"

"If . . . if we really can——" She could not stop the tears any longer. "I thought we'd have some time together. The two of us."

"Yes," he said, "that would have been nice."

She stiffened her shoulders. "I'm sorry. Don't mind me."

He forgot shyness and kissed her lightly on the lips. They did not notice the agents who came around the house, in plain clothes but armed, running in the crouched zigzag of soldiers. Not until an aircar passed overhead, momentarily blocking off the sunlight, did Koskinen see that the enemy had landed.

He had looked forward to some comic relief when they tried to break in, but by the time Vivienne was seated on the low blockhouse roof and smoking a cigarette with some return of coolness, the siege had settled down. Two dozen hard young men ringed the patio with weapons.

Koskinen walked to the invisible wall and tapped his minicom. A man nodded and called something. Koskinen was only mildly surprised when Hugh Marcus himself came from the house with a transceiver on his own wrist.

They confronted each other, a yard apart, an uncrossable few centimeters raised between. Marcus smiled. "Hello, there, Pete," he said.

Coldness surged up: "Mr. Koskinen to you."

"Now you're being childish," Marcus said. "This whole escapade has been so fantastic, in fact, that I can only guess you've gone psycho."

Gently again: "Come on out and let us cure you. For your own sake. Please."

"Cure me of my memory? Or my life?"

"Do stop being so theatrical."

"Where's Dave Abrams?"

"He——"

"Bring my shipmates here," Koskinen said. "You admit you have them. Let them stand immediately outside this barrier. I'll readjust it to include them. If they then tell me you've only kept them for their own protection, I'll come out and beg your humble pardon. Otherwise I'll stay put till the sun freezes."

Marcus reddened. "Do you know what you're doing? You're setting yourself against the government of the United States."

"Oh? How? Perhaps I am guilty of resisting arrest, but I have not committed any treason in the Constitutional sense. Let's take the case to court. My lawyer will argue that the arrest was wrongful. Because you know I haven't done anything to rate it."

"What? Why, your misappropriation of government property——"

"Uh-uh." Koskinen shook his head. "I'm prepared to turn this gadget over to the proper authority at any time. The Astronautical Authority, that is. The articles of the expedition said in plain language——"

Marcus's forefinger lanced out. "Treason, yes! You're withholding something vital to the security of the United States."

"Has Congress passed a law regulating the use

185

of potential barrier fields? Has there even been a Presidential proclamation? Sorry, chum. The articles I signed never said a word about secrecy. Contrariwise. We were expected to publish our findings.''

Marcus stood silent a space, then threw back his head and stated flatly: ''I've got better things to do than argue with an incompetent amateur lawyer. You're under arrest. If you continue to resist, we'll burn you out.''

''Have fun,'' said Koskinen. He walked back to Vivienne. The figures outside ran here and there, and soon three of them returned carrying laser guns.

''So they actually deduced that,'' Vivienne said on a note like terror.

''Sure, I never doubted they would. They're not stupid, much.'' Koskinen slipped down into the pit with her. They settled themselves on the supply pile.

Sunlight filtered through the openings, touching her hair with a crow's wing sheen. His heart thudded as he looked at her. The lasers opened fire and she gripped his hand tightly. But those beams, which could burn through armor plate, were unable to do more than warm the concrete and earth mass of the blockhouse very slightly.

After a while, Marcus's voice said from his minicom: ''Let's talk again.''

''If it amuses you,'' Koskinen answered. ''But on condition you keep those silly heat rays elsewhere.''

''All right,'' Marcus said furiously.

''My partner will stay inside here, in case you do

try to snipe me," Koskinen warned. "She's as stubborn about this business as I am." Not without trepidation, he emerged and went toward Marcus.

The chief looked almost bemused. He ran a hand through his gray hair. "What's your game, Koskinen? What do you want?"

"First, my friends released."

"But they wouldn't be safe!"

"Stop lying. A police escort would be ample for them, if there really is any danger. Since you haven't produced them yet, I know why they're being held and I can make a pretty good guess how most of them have been treated. My second point would make them perfectly safe anyhow, since there'd be no more reason to snatch them. I want the facts about the shield, including how to manufacture one, made public."

"What!" Marcus seemed genuinely aghast, so much so that the agents near him stepped closer. He waved them back and stared at Koskinen. Long gold-colored light fell across both men and glowed on the leaves behind.

"You're crazy," Marcus said. "You don't know what it'd mean."

"So tell me," Koskinen invited.

"Why, every crook would be immune to the police——"

"Wouldn't every honest citizen be immune to the crook? Let this thing be refined further, let it be engineered into a pocketsize gadget which lets you move about freely while the screen is up, and I'd guess there'll be a nearly complete end to personal violence. Confidence men and such can still

187

be arrested, you know, by restraining their movements. It'd be more difficult than now, but the gain to society would justify that."

"Maybe so. But I'll tell you what else it would end." Marcus thrust out his jaw. "The Protectorate. Do you want the atomic wars back?"

"The Protectorate won't be needed any more."

"Can this thing withstand an atomic bomb?"

"N-no. Not a direct hit or a near miss. But a larger unit would be able to. Every city could be equipped with a generator, that would go on automatically when a missile was detected. The only danger would be from bombs smuggled in, and that isn't too hard to guard against, as you well know."

"There are a billion Chinese, Koskinen. A billion—can you understand that number? We sit on the lid only because we could destroy them faster than they could charge us. If our weapons were useless against them——"

"Why, then you'd simply turn on your own barrier field. You won't see hordes marching across the Bering Strait one winter, or sailing across the Pacific, if that's what you're afraid of. They'd be too easy to stop . . . without any shooting, even. A big potential barrier, with the generator anchored to bedrock, would do it."

Koskinen saw Marcus's face change. Could the idea possibly be getting across? Hope flared in him. "Look," he continued, "you're missing the essential point. Not only is war going to become impractical, it isn't even going to be tried. You need a stern government and a regimented populace to organize modern war. And how long do you think any government can last that isn't popular—easygoing—when any citizen can tell his masters to go take a running dive? Don't worry about Wang's dictatorship. Six months from now Wang'll be cowering inside his own barrier field with a mob waiting to starve him out!"

Marcus leaned forward. "Do you realize the same thing could happen here?" he asked most softly.

"Sure," Koskinen said. "And long overdue."

"Do you want anarchy, then?"

"No. Only freedom. Limited government and individual independence. The hard, practical ability of a man to say 'no' when he feels some demand on him—by society or by another individual—is outrageous; and to make his 'no' stick. Wasn't that always the American ideal? There may be some upheaval here and there as the world readjusts, but I'd call that a small price for a return to Jefferson's principles. 'The tree of liberty must be watered from time to time with the blood of patriots and tyrants'——remember? And in this case I don't expect any blood would be shed except the tyrants'."

Koskinen lowered his voice, which had rung out with the old brave words. "I know you hate to see your job made obsolete," he said. "A job you believe in. But you'll have plenty to do, helping the transition along. You'll have more fun, even, in a world that's begun bubbling again, instead of this surly garrison state. Let's be friends, shall we?"

The director stood motionless. A breeze ruffled his hair, and Koskinen wished he too could feel

Earth's air moving over him. The sun slipped low.

Marcus raised his eyes and rasped, "This has gone far enough. If you don't surrender at once, you'll be in real trouble."

Koskinen tried to answer, but couldn't. He swallowed grief and wrath, snapped off his transmission, and went back to Vivienne.

"No go?" she asked. A glow globe lit the bunker, where darkness had already entered. She knelt by some packages she was opening. He shook his head and sat down. Weariness began to drag at him.

"Do eat," she urged. "I'm afraid it isn't the supper I promised you, though. I'll give you a rain check on that."

"I'd like to see rain again," he sighed.

She stopped what she was doing. "Don't you expect to?"

"Oh, I have hopes. Hope is all we've got to go on." He leaned back against the supply pile and stared at his hands.

Vivienne finished her work and made him take some nourishment. "Now lie down for a while," she said. He didn't resist, but laid his head in her lap. Sleep came like a blow.

XX

SHE shook him awake. "Uh," he said, struggling through many thick layers. "Oh . . . ugh. . . . Yeh. You wanna rest?" He knuckled his eyes. The lids felt gritty. "Damn me. I should have let you sleep first."

"That's not the trouble," she said. Her expression was intent in the glow light. "They've brought machinery."

"Oh." Koskinen stuck his head out of the shelter. Floodlamps had been erected, hiding the night in glare. Two movable cranes loomed dinosaurian over the barrier. Their treads had ripped the turf to pieces. Laborers accompanied them.

Koskinen looked at his watch. "Quarter to five," he said. "Took 'em quite a while to fetch that stuff, eh?"

"But what will they do?"

"Didn't I explain this possibility? What we've got here weighs too much to be carried off by hand. They figure to lift us by machines instead.

191

Probably put us in a stratoship and take us some-place more convenient for them.''

''But Pete——'' She leaned against him. He laid an arm around her waist. After a minute he sensed the fear draining from her. ''You don't seem worried,'' she said.

''Lord, no,'' he laughed.

The hooks came down. Chains were attached, harnessing the invisible shell. A foreman waved his crew back. The crane arms began slowly rising.

''Okay,'' Koskinen said. ''Class dismissed.'' He hunkered down by the generator and turned the adjustment knob.

The barrier field expanded a foot, irresistibly. Chains broke in pieces and whipped across the yard. The cranes swayed. Koskinen retracted the field. ''I think I could knock those monsters over by extending our roof upward,'' he said, ''but why risk hurting the operators?''

''You know something?'' Vivienne said shakily. ''You're wonderful.''

The confusion outside settled down again. The workers left with their cranes; the agents resumed guardian positions outside the circle of flood-lighting. Marcus stepped into it, alone.

''Koskinen,'' said his voice from the minicom, as the younger man switched it back on.

''Yes?'' Koskinen stayed where he was. He didn't want to confront Marcus again.

''Pretty good trick, that. Do you plan to keep on resisting?''

''Yes.''

Marcus sighed. ''You leave me no choice.''

Koskinen's vocal cords seized up on him. He waited listening to his heart.

"I hate to do this," Marcus said. "But if you don't come out, I'll have to use an atomic bomb."

Koskinen heard Vivienne's gasp. Her nails dug into his wrist. "You can't," he snarled. "Not without a Presidential order. I know that much law."

"How do you know I don't have an order?"

Koskinen passed a dry tongue across his lips. "Look," he said, "if you can get the President to okay such a thing, you can a lot easier get him to come here and give me his personal assurance you aren't trying to grab all the power there is before the power you've got slips away from you. If he'll do that, I'll come out."

"You'll come out when you're told, Koskinen. This minute."

"In other words, you don't have any Presidential authorization and you know you can't get it. Now who's breaking the law?"

"Military Security has the legal right to use the nuclear weapons in its arsenals, on its own initiative, in case of dire national emergency."

"What's so dire about us? We're only sitting here."

Marcus looked at his watch. "Quarter past five," he said. "You have two hours to surrender." He walked quickly, stiff-legged, from the light.

"Pete." Vivienne shuddered against Koskinen. "He's bluffing, isn't he? He can't. Not for real."

"I'm afraid he can," Koskinen said.

"But how can he explain it afterwards?"

"Trump up some story or other. There won't be any evidence left, you know. Plenty of fireball atoms travel fast enough to penetrate this shield, not to mention radiant heat. Obviously his men here are a hand-picked core, loyal to him rather than to the Constitution. Every would-be dictator recruits such a gang, according to all the sociology I ever studied. So they'll support his yarn. Sure, he can get away with it."

"But he'll lose the generator too!"

"That's better than losing his position, and his chance for a still higher position. Besides, he may figure that his tame scientists now have clues which'll let them work out the secret in time."

"Pete, there isn't any secret! We took care of that. Why haven't you told him?"

"Because I was afraid, I still am, that he'd fire that bomb at once. We, right here, with a working potential barrier machine, we're the only immediate proof that he's a liar and traitor who's outlived his day. No one can make a unit overnight, you realize. The first handmade prototypes can't be ready for days at best. If he acts fact, knowing the situation, Marcus's gang still has a chance to hunt down the people we contacted, and brand everything as an anti-Protectorate conspiracy. But that's provided the rest of the government believes him and backs him. Which they won't as long as we're able to testify."

"I see," she said. After a moment, for no reason he could guess, she switched off the glow globe. The blaze outside was softened as it diffused through the shelter entrance, until it touched her with highlights and embracing shadows. "We can only wait, then," she said.

"Maybe your Brazilian friend, that you phoned the whole story to, maybe he'll be able to get action in time."

"Maybe. He's had to go through a lot of bureaucratic channels if he's accomplished anything so far. And his own government has him on the 'suspicious' list because he knew Johnny. Still, he is a journalist. He should know more ropes than most people."

"How about that Senator you mentioned? The one you said is a libertarian."

"Hohenrieder? Yes, I told him too, as well as sending him a set of plans. But it wasn't him I talked to, of course. A secretary, who looked skeptical. Maybe he wiped the tape at once. Hohenrieder's office must get a lot of crank calls."

"Still, maybe the guy did pass this one on to his boss. So there's your Brazilian journalist certainly trying to tell the President of the U.S. what's going on, and Senator Hohenrieder possibly trying, and maybe a few of the others, who've simply gotten our standard message, have put two and two together and are also trying. They may succeed at any minute."

"Cut out that fake cheerfulness, darling," she said. "I'm perfectly well able to face the fact that they probably won't succeed before 0715. Marcus may be in jail by noon; but we'll never know."

"Maybe not," he admitted reluctantly. After a second: "We're better off than we were in the Zodiac, anyhow. This won't hurt. You won't feel a thing."

"I know. In a way, that scares me worst. Life has so suddenly begun to matter again."

"Do you want to go out to them?" he asked. "I can switch off the barrier for half a second and you can run out."

"Lord, no!" Her vehemence put life back in them both. She laughed unsteadily and groped about for a cigarette.

"I love you, you see," he floundered.

"And I think I love you. So is there a way to—"

"Maybe not. Not when I realize you may be dead in a hundred minutes. I wouldn't be able to forget that. I wouldn't know how to forget, how to do anything right. I'd rather love you the way I do understand, talking, or simply looking at you. Can you see, Veevee?" he said in his wretchedness.

"I think so," she answered at last, infinitely gently.

"And there may, after all, be another time for us," he said, attempting to sound eager. Then I'll be asking you!"

He did not know why pain crossed her face. But she smiled and nestled beside him. They held hands. Afterward he remembered that the talking had been mostly his, about what they would do in their future together.

The first sunlight tinged the sky. They went outside to watch, careless of heat ray snipers, looking past the guards who still stood in shadow, even past the ugly long cylinder that had been wheeled on a cart next to the barrier field.

"Sunrise," Koskinen said, "trees, flowers, the

river, but mostly you. I'm glad I came back to Earth.''

She didn't reply. He could not keep from looking at his watch. The time was 0647.

A bullet spray chewed holes in the house wall. Koskinen jumped. The Security car which had been hovering on guard sped away. A gleaming needle swept after it. Guns flashed fire. The car staggered and fell downward. Koskinen didn't see it strike, but smoke puffed up above the trees.

The slender craft returned. "That's Air Force!" Koskinen screamed. "The insignia, see, Air Force——''

A man in uniform came running and dodging through the flowerbeds. An MS agent dropped to one knee and shot at him with a submachine gun. The soldier hit dirt just beneath the bullet stream. His arm chopped through an arc. Koskinen saw the grenade coming. Instinctively, he thrust Vivienne behind him. Not even sound penetrated the barrier. But at least, he realized with nausea, he had spared her a view of the agent's death. The others scattered from sight.

No—one man pelted over the torn grass. Marcus! His face was twisted out of humanness; slaver ran from his mouth. He reached the bomb and fumbled with its nose. A soldier dashed from behind a willow tree and fired. Marcus went on his belly. The soldier approached, turned him over, shook a helmeted head and looked warily around. Marcus's dead eyes glared at the rising sun.

There was no more fighting that Koskinen saw. He held Vivienne close, wondering why she sobbed. An Army platoon deployed around the potential shell. He read nothing on their young faces except amazement.

A grizzled man led three or four junior officers and a couple of civilians around the house and onto the patio. Four stars gleamed on his shoulders. "Koskinen?" he said into his minicom. He stopped, peering uncertainly at the two behind the barrier.

"Yes?" Koskinen remembered to switch on his own transmitter. "Hello?"

"I'm General Grahovitch. Regular Army——" a contemptuous glance at Marcus's corpse—— "Special Operations office. Here by Presidential command. We only came to investigate, but when we landed, these birds opened fire. What the devil *is* the situation?"

"I'll explain," said Koskinen. "One minute, please." He unwrapped Vivienne's arms from around his neck, sprang into the shelter and turned off the generator. As he came out, the dawn wind blew across him.

XXI

HE had a moment alone with her in the living room, by grace of General Grahovitch, before they embarked for Washington. As he entered, he saw her at a window, staring out across the lawn to the river and the hills beyond.

"Veevee," he said.

She didn't turn. He came behind her, laid his hands on her waist and said into her ear, with the blue-black hair tickling his lips and smelling like summer, "Everything's settled. All over but the shouting."

Still she didn't move.

"Of course," he said, "the shouting's apt to last quite a while. I'm told that half the government officials who've heard the news think I ought to be hanged for scattering the plans around so widely. But the other half sees that we really had very little choice and didn't break any important laws, so the only thing to do is accept the *fait accompli* and make heroes of us. I can't say I relish that prospect, but we should be able to sneak off eventually.''

''That's good,'' she said in a flat voice.

He kissed her cheek. ''And then——'' he said shyly.

''Oh, yes,'' she said. ''I don't doubt you'll have a wonderful time.''

''What do you mean, me? I'm thinking about us.'' He grew aware of the tension under his hands. ''Hey, you aren't worried about those old charges, are you? I have Grahovitch's personal word that you'll get not just a pardon, but a national apology.''

''It was good of you to remember about me, in the middle of everything else,'' she said. Slowly, forcing herself, she turned about and met his gaze. ''I'm not surprised, though. You're that kind of guy.''

''Nuts,'' he blustered. ''Got to take care of my own wife, don't I? Uh——'' He saw with uncomprehending shock that she was not crying simply because she had wept herself dry.

''I'll miss you like anything, Pete,'' she said.

''What are you talking about?''

''You don't think I'd tie a man like you . . . to somebody like me . . . do you? I haven't sunk that far.''

''What do you mean, sunk? Don't you want me? That time——before sunrise——''

''That was different,'' she said. ''I didn't expect we'd live. So why not give each other what we could? But for a lifetime? No. It'd be too one-sided.''

''Don't you think I'm anything at all?''

"Oh, Pete, Pete." She took his head between her hands. "Can't you see? It's the other way around. After everything I've done and been——"

"Do you think that matters to me?"

"——everything I still am; because habits don't go away just by my wishing they would. Yes, it does matter. Not now; you're still too young to understand. But later it would. As the years passed. As you came to know me better, and know other people too, people like Leah Abrams, and started realizing—— No. I can't do that to you. Or to myself, even. Let's say a clean goodbye."

"But what will you do?" he asked, stunned into stupidity, seeing only afterward that the one rational thing might perhaps have been to prevent her by force from departing.

"I'll manage," she said. "My kind always does. I'll disappear——I know how to do that very thoroughly——and get a new face somewhere, and find something to keep me busy. Remember, darling, how short a time you've known me. In six months you'll have trouble recalling what I looked like. I know. I've known so many."

She kissed him, a hasty gesture, as if she were afraid. "But next to Johnny," she said, "I liked you the best."

Before he could stir, she was out the door, walking down toward the riverside where several Army aircars waited. Her head was held high.

POUL ANDERSON
Masterpieces of Science Fiction